51 Ways To End Your *World*

By

Charis Emanon

MONTAG

First Montag Press E-Book and Paperback Original Edition February 2022

Copyright © 2022 by Charis Emanon

As the writer and creator of this story, Charis Emanon asserts the right to be identified as the author of this book.

Montag Press ISBN: 978-1-957010-04-5
Design © 2022 Amit Dey

Montag Press Team:
Cover Artist: Renato Pinto
Editor: Charlie Franco

A Montag Press Book
www.montagpress.com
Montag Press
777 Morton Street, Unit B
San Francisco CA 94129 USA

Montag Press, the burning book with the hatchet cover, the skewed word mark and the portrayal of the long-suffering fireman mascot are trademarks of Montag Press.

Printed & Digitally Originated in the United States of America
10 9 8 7 6 5 4 3 2 1

This book is a work of fiction. Names, characters, places, and incidents are either products of the author's vivid and sometimes disturbing imagination or are used fictitiously without any regards with possible parallel realities. Any resemblance to actual persons, living or dead, events, or locales is entirely coincidental.

Advance Reviews for
51 Ways To End Your World:

"Emanon's arresting characters have been vacuum-packed into an apocalyptic kaleidoscope. His down-to-earth observations during the endtimes tumble effortlessly from the page into the reader's heart, and it strikes me as the most humanitarian book on death that I've read in some time. A graphic sketch of human communication: a novel of genial, genuine disaster whose uncomplicated brilliance both eulogizes the present and brightens the dark. Profound and unsettling."

— **Walker Zupp,** author of *Martha*

"How many apocalypses can one world take? *51 Ways To End Your World* is a fast-paced novel of a world turned upside down and inside out. Junior-college student Anna Frod just wants to be left alone to peacefully die from lack of sleep, but the violently disintegrating world is in danger of rescue. She must put aside her personal needs and meet the challenge: stop a villainous scientist from saving the world. The breezy, tongue-in-cheek narrative perfectly counterpoints this biting satire of modern America's skewed values and dysfunctional obsessions. Thoroughly entertaining!"

— **Kathy L. Brown,** author of *The Big Cinch*

"Emanon tosses the reader into a carnival of satiric mayhem in his novel, *51 Ways To End Your World.* Characters stumble through catastrophe as if lost in the funhouse. In Emanon's world, disaster is uncontainable; the Cascade volcanoes erupt simultaneously, changing not only the landscape, but the climate of the entire planet. And how do people respond? With spasms of something you could only call Apocalyptic Insanity Disorder. A witty and entertaining book."

— James M. Wright,
author of *Rhizome, The Gorge of Despair,*
and *The Kraken Imaginary*

"Amazing, a real page turner, great dialog, enjoyable to the max! This is super bone chilling for us PNW residents. Yikes!!"

— Scott Meredith,
author of *Nagendra* and *Astral Advice Animal: The Insider's Reincarnation Playbook*

"*Dr. Strangelove* for whatever bastardized agglomeration of generations we live in. *51 Ways To End Your World* is a sleepwalker falling through a trap door, grabbing you by the ankles to pull you down into the roaring abyss below. Immediate and immersive in its grip, this is a novel that demands attention and rewards it in the most impactful of ways. It sinks its hooks in fast, and once it's through with you, leaves you battered and confused but somehow certain that you are exactly where you're supposed to be.

The absurdity of the thing is scary, but not nearly as scary as just how perfectly timely and relevant it is to the modern world."

— **Paul d. Miller,** author of *Albrecht Drue, ghostpuncher.* and *Albrecht Drue, Paranormal Dick*

"A tragic comedy; a biting satire; the world observed through a twisted lens; *51 Ways To End Your World* is all of these and more. Considering the disaster of epic proportions that it deals with it is studded with sparkling comedic passages while at the same time displaying an acute eye for observation and detail. Among the several threads of the narrative I particularly liked that of the suicidal Anna."

— **Pete Peru,** author of *The Reeking Hegs*

DEDICATION

Dedicated to Christine, Christiana,
and Dallas: you are my first dream and my last.

Author's Preface

Dear Fellow Traveler,

I am honored that you have chosen to read my creation. You summoned this book into existence. We writers are nothing without readers.

After our journey together I would be gratified if you could take the time to share your opinion of my work on Amazon and Goodreads. If you like this novel, please let your friends know on social media and request that your local library purchase a copy so this experience can be shared. While you are at it, won't you friend me on Facebook?

Thank you for taking the time to imagine this story together! I hope you receive as much joy from reading it as I have been given in writing it.

Sincerely,
Charis Emanon

I - Gentle Comes that Good Night

ruth requires one to believe.

Anna found the onset of death to be arousing. Perhaps it was the four lattes that had her wired as she pursued suicide by sleep deprivation. Or it was the little yellow pills. Mostly though, it was the fact that something—at long last—was going to happen. She had been up for 22 hours and 4 minutes straight, and the excitement still hadn't worn off. Anna was going to do something that her psychology textbook only hinted at—she was going to die due to lack of sleep. At 22 hours and 13 minutes, some of the thrill started to wear thin. To fend off sleep, Anna had decided she'd better do something to keep busy. It was at this point that she hit upon the idea of a suicide note. It was something of a traditional touch, but somehow it just felt right. Anna thought it might help to cement the feeling that she was really going through with it this time—that she was really approaching death.

She searched the apartment for paper. Most of her writing for her college classes had been done on the laptop her boyfriend had built for her; Anna hadn't used notebook paper in a while. But a suicide note on college-ruled writing paper seemed best. All she could find, however, was a left-over napkin from Lizzy's Pizza Buffet and reams of printer paper. For a few moments, this setback made Anna want to call the whole thing off. After she recovered from this disappointment, she found she was still sufficiently motivated to continue her suicide attempt. She thought about writing the suicide note on the napkin. The Lizzy's Pizza logo turned her off of this idea. She certainly didn't want her suicide to be turned into free advertising. Instead, she brought out her laptop, hooked it up to the printer, and started typing. She began with the following words:

I, Anna Frod, being a B+ student in Mr. Caretz's Psych 101, have decided to kill myself by way of sleep deprivation. I'm doing this partially because I've been a little depressed lately—also I have been extremely bored. But, mostly, I just want to prove my boyfriend wrong, because he says I'll fall into a coma and not die, while our Coontz textbook indicates that I will die after about 9 days without sleep.

Anna added a signature block and started the date. "This is probably the most important day of my life!" she realized, with a sudden surge of joy at the prospect of making history. She typed "200" and then stopped. For some reason, her mind froze. Anna couldn't remember the date. She scrambled to find her college planner. Looking at the dates there, Anna realized that she hadn't yet written her psych final review paper.

"It was due yesterday!" she exclaimed to no one. The end of the day was the end of the term, and the beginning of Spring Break—by then it would be too late.

Since she had already started typing, Anna transitioned into a technically perfect, if somewhat uninspired, 5-part essay for the rest of the page. In it, she defined sleep deprivation and then proceeded to provide examples of people who had set records for going without sleep—most notably some 17-year-old kid, by the name of Randy Gardner, who had lasted 11 days.

Anna wrapped up the paper and printed it out. It was just about right, she figured. Most of it came word-for-word from the Coontz textbook, but that had never counted against her in this class in the past. Mr. Caretz was one of those cool teachers who just gave everyone at least a B as long as you didn't miss too much class or give him a hard time. He was nothing like that hard-assed Sparnell who had flunked Anna out of her psychology class just because he caught Anna copying a few paragraphs from some Internet article.

Once the paper had printed, Anna threw on some tennis shoes to go with her sweat suit so she could head into downtown Portland to turn in her work. Herald Junior College was due to close within the next couple of hours, this Friday. A few minutes later, she was standing out front of her Gateway apartment waiting for a MAX.

There are several socially observed conventions when it comes to waiting for a light rail surface train. The first, of course, is that you don't stand on the tracks to wait for the train. Despite the fact that she was committing suicide, Anna still complied with this one.

She had once seen a bicyclist hit by one of the trains—or at least she had seen what remained of a bicyclist after he had been dragged a few feet. Up until that point, Anna had always sort of secretly hoped that one of those jerks on a bicycle would wind up getting hit; but, after having seen it once, she decided that she should be more careful about what she wished.

Her second rule was that you never walk between someone waiting for the train and the track. Anna was quickly annoyed as some couple did exactly this. That very same couple then immediately proceeded to break rule three: no physical contact. They sat down on a bench and began to make out.

It wasn't that Anna was a prude or anything—after all, she was "living in sin" with her boyfriend. It was just that the bench was directly beneath the little screen that told when the MAX was due to arrive. To look at it, she had to look straight in the direction of this couple. That made it almost look like she was staring at them; which, of course, would have been a violation of rule four. So Anna had to stand there and sneak side-long glances at the scrolling marquee, which made it look like she was committing the worst sort of violation of rule number four. It made her feel like some sort of creepy peeping tom, which made her hate the couple all the more. She hated them so much that she almost broke rule number five. She almost pulled out her cell phone to make an obnoxiously loud call to her boyfriend while pretending that no one else could hear her. Pretty much everyone nowadays seems to break rule number five.

Before she had a chance to continue any further with this thought, the MAX pulled up in front of her. Just as she had planned, because if she stood on the crack in the cement diagonally cut between the potted tree and the garbage bin, the train stopped with the front doors directly in front of her. Anna knew that getting in through these doors first would put her in a good position to reach the front corner chair—a single seat that faced the back of the driver's cabin, where she wouldn't have to look at any other passengers—before anyone else could get there.

Unfortunately, this was when some scruffy guy wearing an old army field jacket broke rule number six. He darted in front of Anna and burst through the sliding doors first. While she paused to avoid making physical contact with this stranger—which would have violated rule number two, the couple that had already violated rules two and three squeezed past Anna. Astounded by the fact that three rules had already been broken by this same couple, Anna stomped onto the train herself.

It looked like she was still in luck because the entire front cabin of the train was pretty much empty and Anna's prized front corner seat was still available. She followed the rule-breaking couple up the aisle toward the front of the train, waiting for her chance to slide past them and into her coveted seat. Then the couple had the audacity to break rule number fifteen. Well, it wasn't a rule before this point, but Anna had added it after this incident. The woman sat in the single corner seat, with the man on her lap—and they immediately went back to kissing!

This was too much. Anna slumped into one of the paired seats behind the couple, directly next to a window. As she did so, she felt someone else sit down in the aisle seat beside hers. She looked up in time to see army-jacket man taking up residence in that seat. This despite the fact that empty seats were all around them: a clear violation of rule seven.

She then violated rule number eight; she stared directly into the man's eyes so as to signal to him just how great her hatred for him was. He seemed to take this as a sign of interest and appeared ready to open his mouth to speak to her—which would have broken rule nine. Anna quickly looked away to try to head off this outcome. She turned to face forward and found herself staring directly at the make-out couple, thus breaking rule four once more. The woman saw Anna's glance and whispered something to the man between passionate kisses. Anna wasn't sure what was said, but she was pretty sure she heard the phrase "perverts on this train."

She turned to face the window. On this part of the journey, there was nothing to see from the ravine through which the train shot except for the backs of hillside apartment buildings, warehouses, and the occasional homeless campsite set up in the bushes. But, when the train moved through a tunnel, she was able to catch her reflection.

Her acne had cleared up quite a bit. It barely showed up around the tip of her forehead and just below the point on the right side of her face where a black triangle patch of her hair dipped in front of her ear. She liked her new haircut, even though her boyfriend had complained that it made her look "too much like a boy." It probably hadn't helped matters that Anna had shot back, "I could say the same about you!"

And there, just behind the pointed hood of her sweat top, was Anna's wrinkled and hairy hand, resting on the…

Wait a second, that's not my hand! Anna thought as she realized that army-jacket was slowly working his hand across the bar on the back of their pair of seats and toward her shoulder.

That would have been a major violation of rules three, ten, and possibly fourteen—Anna had lost track by this point. She turned towards the man and glared once more. As the train came to a complete stop, briefly opening its doors, closing them again, and then started once more, she kept up her hateful stare.

He leered back. He ran his tongue around his cracked lips. From out of the hairy hole that formed his mouth, words arose. They entered the air and drifted toward Anna in slow motion.

"Pretty fine day for a pretty little thing like you, ain't it," he said with a wink.

"Excuse me," Anna said, as she stood up and began to force her way past him. "This is my stop."

He didn't move at all, forcing Anna to push past him to make it to the aisle. She felt his fleshy knees press into her thighs.

"Yeah, you'll get what you deserve…" she heard the man whisper, as she moved away and the train lurched toward its downtown stops.

She stared straight ahead, pretending not to hear. Anna kept this up for stop after stop, as snatches of the man's muttered comments, intertwined with accusations of "liar!" drifted toward her.

Finally, the train screeched to a halt at the corner of Morrison and Broadway. As she stumbled toward the doors, wishing they would slide open more quickly, she thought she heard the hairy ape mumble, "There's a place in hell for a bitch like you …"

She pushed her way through the incoming crowds at the Pioneer Square Stop and out onto the MAX platform. She rushed across the street and toward a high-rise building, between the Nordstrom and Banana Republic, with a big neon front piece that formed the words *Herald Junior College*.

At the end of an alley, just before the front doors of the college, sat a teenaged girl—complete with a nose ring, knapsack, and a Doberman pinscher on a leash. She sat with her arms wrapped around her knees, pulled tight against her chest.

"Spare change today?" the girl called out.

"Sorry, I don't have any pockets."

"You got pockets on your sweatshirt," the girl corrected Anna.

"Yeah," Anna replied, as she pushed open the glass front doors to the building. "That's just my bus pass and assignment. Listen, I'm sorry, but I'm late…"

She hurried toward the elevators and pressed the *Up* button on the wall between them. Soon she was at the college's front desk on the second floor.

"I've got this assignment to leave for my teacher, Mr. Caretz," she told the receptionist. "I don't know where he's at for his office hours…"

"Oh, Caretz," the man at the front desk replied. "Yeah, he doesn't keep regular office hours. He'll show up sooner or later—don't worry; I'll get this to him."

Having completed her major task for the day, Anna was at a loss for what to do next. Since there were still a few hours of daylight, she headed for the student lounge on the third floor. She ordered an extra-tall latte from a vendor's cart and took it out to the patio. She plopped down into a lawn chair and sat there in the sunlight and stared off across the city.

She looked up the hillside and towards the cathedral that stood at the center of Oregon's Portland University. That was where Anna had first gone to school before Sparnell had her thrown out for cheating. Anna missed being a student at the larger college. There, everyone drank coffee, smoked cigarettes, and talked about the "real world" as if it existed in a universe far away. Herald Junior College, on the other hand, was just a place inbetween—either between high school and "real" college or between a dead-end job and a hoped-for career. None of her classmates had much time to play the role of student, between kids, groceries, and rent. Their world was already far too real and Anna hated that world.

Anna had been awake for 24 hours and 33 minutes. She wondered how long until the arrival of her death. Already strange things seemed to be happening; her vision was clouding up. Everything was getting dark. The psychology textbook had talked about hallucinations; Anna wondered—and sort of hoped—that this was the beginning of the first one. Before she could think more about this, she sensed someone standing behind her. She looked up and saw Mr. Caretz looking down at her.

"Good afternoon, Ms. Frod," he said, and then stopped to clear his throat. "I thought I saw you down here. The receptionist just handed me your paper and I was about to go over it. Let's see what it says here…"

Caretz droned on while he took a pair of glasses out of the pocket of his vest and put them on his face. With his other hand, he pulled her folded-up paper out of the front pocket of his pants and set it on the glass surface of a little round table that stood nearby.

"Let's see," he began, as he ran his fat palm through the thinning hair at the crown of his forehead. "… a B+ student … have decided to…"

Caretz looked up in alarm. His words came out in bursts.

"You've decided to kill yourself! Because of my class! No, no, I'm up for review! How long have you been awake? I've got to get you some sleeping pills—I've got a bottle in my office. We'll just pour a bunch of those into you and everything…"

As he spoke, Caretz seemed to slowly fade away. Anna watched him drift off, the blackness swirling all around her. Just then, the world began to shake, and she heard a high-pitched noise, a shriek.

···✦✦◆✦✦···

Ben wished he was gay.

Everything would have been much better if he had been. He wanted so badly for it to be so—as he waited there at Portland International Airport's Gate C with his Army National Guard unit. After all, everyone else in the unit already thought he was gay. Ben just didn't fit in with them—with his constant reading and writing. He could have gotten away with the reading during long drill weekends if he had stuck to Tom Clancy novels, survivalist paraphernalia, or Penthouse letters. But he spent time reading things like *Babbit*, *The Brothers K*, and—the clincher, as far as his unit was concerned—*Jane Eyre*. Of course, writing in a journal certainly didn't help.

Ben was used to it. All of his life, because his last name nearly rhymed with a certain word, he'd been teased for being gay. When he had gone to Basic Training out at Fort Benning it had only been a matter of time before his drill sergeants and fellow soldiers picked up the taunt. Bigotry wasn't usually all that original Ben had found.

"Hey, faggot—I got you something."

The red-haired soldier closed in on where the fatigue-clad Ben sat atop an olive green backpack. He and his giggling comrades formed a semicircle around him. He looked up at the other soldier, coldly eyeing him and the ogling pair that stood with him.

"I told you the name is Padgett. Specialist Padgett to you, Private."

"Yeah, whatever—I bet you'd love to see *my* privates. It's a present, something to keep you company as we head out for AT in California."

The private pulled a magazine out from underneath his army issue brown t-shirt and tossed it at Ben. It landed just in front of his black boots.

"You bought *this* for me," Ben said, picking up the Playgirl magazine. He ignored their burst of laughter as he continued, "And you bought *this* here in the airport, right Rieck?"

"Yeah … that's right," the red-haired soldier shot back.

"Well, it just happens that they've got this entire airport covered by cameras, ever since 9-11—including the airport shops. Did these guys see you buy the magazine? I'll even bet there's a clerk that can testify about it too."

"Testify … What exactly are you getting at?" Rieck replied, less confidently now. His face was beginning to turn red.

"Well, Private Rieck, I'm just saying that we've got witnesses and security footage of you buying a Playgirl magazine… This is a magazine with naked men in it, right? Don't you think Uncle Sam's Army will think it's kind of queer, you buying a magazine full of naked men and all?"

As he spat out these words, Ben rolled up the magazine and tossed it back at Rieck. It hit him across the face.

"I think you had better find some place to hide that magazine, don't you? I've got a few places I'd like to suggest you stick it if you can't figure it out."

Rieck hastily grabbed up the magazine as he and his comrades retreated. He stuck the magazine back beneath his t-shirt before he turned to toss one last threat Ben's way.

"Don't worry, Padgett. We're going to have two weeks to play out there."

Padgett knew that was true. He had joined the army because he had wanted to help fight floods and fires like his dad had done back when he had joined the Oregon Army National Guard. But nowadays the Army had the National Guard units constantly preparing for wars in the Middle East and Korea, which meant less time among real people and more time drilling in the field—all of which meant Ben got to spend most of his time with 'true' patriots like Rieck.

As he boarded the civilian plane, Padgett felt sick to his stomach. He had signed up for the National Guard because it was only a weekend a month and two weeks obligation every summer. But he'd quickly discovered that time in the military—with its 5 am to 1 am work days, and "hurry up and wait" training philosophy—went much more slowly than time back at his job at the B and M One-Stop Grocery Outlet. To top it all off, he had to contend with constant hostility from his homophobic comrades in arms.

The more he protested that he wasn't gay, the more the accusations flew. It didn't help that he had a pasty face and a high-pitched voice. It certainly didn't help that he was bored by shooting rifles and didn't like to watch things explode.

It all made Ben wonder if it wasn't all true—maybe he was gay and just didn't know it. He had tried to think gay for a while. During showers in the barracks, he would sneak looks at his comrades to see if he felt any sort of reaction—which, of course, hadn't helped his cause as far as his fellow soldiers were concerned. He tried to admire the shapely male bodies, the young muscular physiques. But all he saw was a bunch of hairy, sweaty, pimply bodies. Nothing moved him.

Still, Ben had never really been attracted to girls, either—and it appeared to be a reciprocal deal. So Ben lived his life in a kind of confusion that grew more encompassing every time he was forced to deal with the other soldiers on drill weekends.

Back at AIT, he had thought about discussing the topic with the unit chaplain, a mild man known as Colonel Drayner. Then he found out that the last soldier that had done so—after having been assured by Drayner that he was speaking in confidence—had had his name turned into the Army's elite "Morale and Integrity" Investigation team. The MI Unit seized all of the soldier's possessions (in search of proof of immoral conduct), looked the other way when his platoon held a blanket party for the soldier, and then had him drummed out of the military under a discharge that was categorized as "other than honorable." Once the soldier was gone, Colonel Drayner had led the entire company in a prayer of thanksgiving.

Ben's thoughts on this topic were interrupted as the pilot's voice filled the cabin. With a start, he realized that the commercial plane was already in the air and he turned to look out his wing-side window to see what the pilot was describing.

"...off to the southeast of us you'll see Mt. Hood and we're circling north towards Mt. St. Helens as we gain cruising altitude. It appears that Mt. St. Helens is going to put on a little show for us—you can see a small puff of ash and steam coming out right now. It's nothing to be alarmed about—you locals know that it has done this on and off ever since the big one back in 1980."

A thick black cloud was rising out of the crater of the mountain. The black poured over the mountain's rim and was already beginning to cover the valley, starting at the north with the city of Vancouver, between the mountain and the Columbia River.

Then, a bright orange glow appeared on the upper lip on the southern side of the mountain and the entire sky was plunged into darkness.

"That's bigger than a small puff," the woman in the seat behind Ben said. "Is this plane shaking or is it the mountain that's moving?!"

As if he'd heard her question, the pilot's voice came back over the cabin's speakers, "That looks to be a lot bigger eruption than what those folks in the tower were talking about! Is that ash hitting us? It looks like we're flying through dirt … or rocks! Oh God, those are boulders hitting us! We've been hit… we've got to get this thing back on the ground, now!"

Ben could feel the plane bouncing sideways as it was pelted in the darkness. Passengers started screaming. It felt like the plane's cabin was being sucked free of air.

Ben's skin broke into a thick sweat as a loud buzzing rang out, his fingers curled tightly around the back of the seat in front of him. He couldn't see a thing through the darkness out his window.

"Oh God—we're not going to make it!"

The captain's screech carried across the plane's speakers. The screams from the passengers grew louder as the plane's shaking became stronger.

"What do you mean it's still on? I could replace this entire crew with monkeys and get better…" the captain's voice began and then cut out.

A moment later, a new voice came across the speakers, "Ladies and gentlemen, I hope you are enjoying your flight with us today. We are experiencing some unexpected turbulence, but the captain has it all under control. We would, however, like to request that you close the shade on your windows at this point. There is nothing out there to see of interest—just sit back and relax… What do you mean, there are only 3 parachutes! You'd better give me…"

The speakers shut down again as the cabin went pitch black. Sparks began to shoot out of one of the overhead panels. The screams were drowned out by a high-pitched whine from the wing beside where Ben sat. An acrid scent filled Ben's nostrils. One of the plane's oxygen masks dropped down in front of him.

···◆ ◆ ◆ ◆···

Eddie Chandran wanted to design buildings. He wanted to create houses and office buildings that people would come to see and say, "That's a Chandran." He wanted to do these things, but he had learned that he wasn't able to do them because he was no good at math or physics and was never going to score high enough on the tests to get into an architectural or engineering program. It would be his fault, he supposed. After all, his older brothers had all gone on to prestigious universities—all of them were computer programmers, string theorists, and the like. But all the way through school, from the very beginning, Eddie had known he was different from them.

For the first years, all of the other students in the American public schools had tried to sneak a peek at his answers during math tests. After all, everyone knows that India has a long history with mathematics—his native country had practically invented the stuff. But, after flunking a few tests, the other children knew that it was no use to copy the answers off of Chandran. He was hopeless when it came to math.

"I'll bet he's not even a real Indian," Eddie once overheard one of the girls telling her friends out by the tether ball court. "I don't think he could even do a rain dance or take a scalp."

"Maybe I'm not a real Indian," Eddie had thought.

Perhaps he was too much of an American to be good at math. It made some sense, since he was the youngest of five brothers and the only one who had never attended school in India.

His family had decided to move to America back when Eddie was only four years old. He still remembered the day his father had made the decision.

"Look at that Naipaul. Those Southern Baptists began sponsoring him—they put his picture on posters in all of their Sunday Schools in America. The next thing you know, he has American nickels, dimes, and quarters rolling in every week. He got a good house, the dowry to get a good wife, a good donkey, and his own movie screen. I bet those American children have no idea they are sending money to a 40-year-old man who spends half of it on prostitutes! I'm going to get one of my sons on those posters so we can make enough money to move to America; then we'll tell those children to stop sending money to that fraud Naipaul!"

That was exactly what Eddie's father, Biswas, had done. First, he had gone to the Southern Baptist missionaries. He explained that he and his family would like to convert to Southern Baptism if only one of his children could be sponsored by their organization much as Naipaul had been.

The Southern Baptists thanked Biswas for his interest but explained that the children of America only felt comfortable giving money to the picture of Naipaul as a five-year-old. Besides, it would cost a great deal to make up new posters. And, anyhow, back in America the Southern Baptists were busy contemplating boycotting Disney World; so there wasn't all that much interest in taking on new converts in light of such pressing concerns.

Biswas next tried the Seventh Day Adventists, Latter Day Saints, Church of the Mother of Pearl, Reformed Anabaptist Calvinists, and the First Church of the People's National Heritage. All of these groups either already had a poster child—or were too busy with the opium trade to be interested in saving the souls of heathens from hell. Finally, Biswas received a positive response from the Lutheran missionaries (not the ELCA wing, or the SDL version, but the LCMS group). They did have an opening for an Indian poster child; but they wanted a girl to do the job. So Eddie's older brother, Willie, had worn a pretty little dress, and the sponsorship deal went through.

That had gotten the family to America. For his brothers, the change of countries had worked out well. They now all had government jobs or tenured professorships at major universities. But Eddie had often wondered if his own life wouldn't have turned out better if he had grown up in India. All that he had managed to scare up in the way of a job after high school was a position as a go-getter on a construction crew. Sure, it let him feel like he was within reach of living out his dreams of creating buildings. He got to fetch blueprints for the real architects and serve coffee to the clients who had come to inspect their new buildings.

It was all hard work—and mostly unrelated to what Eddie wanted to do with his life. Much of the job was his chance to be bullied by construction workers who had, in turn, been bullied by those who had trained them. There was a definite pecking order with which to contend, and it would take years of watching and learning before Eddie would ever be allowed to take part in any real construction activity on this crew—he wasn't yet even allowed near the power tools. And he could never hope to design buildings.

"Hey, you … don't be daydreaming on my nickel!"

Eddie looked up in surprise to see who was talking to him. It was a rotund man wearing an orange hard hat, a tool belt, and a sleeveless flannel shirt, who was approaching. He was carrying a bucket full of a tar-like substance dripping down one side.

"I need you to set this bucket up there," the man said. "At the top of the cross beams. Can you handle that?"

"Yes sir!" Eddie said as he grabbed the bucket and began to run towards the ladders. He had quickly learned that it was best to just do exactly as told if you wanted to avoid any screaming.

"Hey, kid… Don't forget your hard hat. We're going to have Camas city inspectors here today, and I don't want them having to step through bits of your brain."

"Yes, right. I'll get it."

Within minutes, Eddie got his hard hat on and was working his way up the ladders carrying the slopping bucket. A crowd had gathered below him while he climbed.

"Hey, try to get some of that slop up to the top, will you!" one of the workers called out. "I don't need it spilled all over my ladders."

As Eddie lifted the bucket over his head, some of the stuff splashed onto the lenses of his glasses. He set the bucket on one of the metal rungs and then used the back of his hand to wipe the glasses clean. He didn't seem to have done a very good job, because everything still was black.

"Hurry up, will ya," another one of the men called from below. "My mother could climb scaffolding quicker than you do!"

"I bet your mother had a lot of experience at mounting things," Eddie thought, but he kept his mouth shut.

He concentrated on lifting his lean body onto the top of the frame. He put the bucket's wire handle in his mouth and then he stood atop the beam. He stretched out his arms as he balanced himself. He had to step carefully because his glasses were cloudy. No longer able to see, he felt his way using the soles of his feet. Slowly, he felt his way along, making sure he kept his balance. It was strangely quiet. The rest of the crew seemed to have given up on giving him advice. Eddie wondered if he was more scared up on this beam than he had realized. His body was breaking into a sweat. He thought he might be having some sort of panic attack. Everything was turning black.

Then, he started to shake. As he shook, the beam below him shook. The shaking became more violent. Eddie knew the men below would yell at him, but he had no choice. He opened his mouth, released the metal handle from the grip he had on it with his teeth, and let the bucket drop. As it fell, it made a splashing sound rather than the solid crash he had expected.

Then the shaking stopped and Eddie was able to balance himself. He had no idea where he was going, everything was shrouded in darkness. He knew from memory that he must be nearing the corner of the beam where a platform had been erected. The rest of the construction crew hadn't yet started yelling at him for dropping the bucket. All he heard was a roaring sound below. Eddie felt for the plywood sheet of the platform below his feet. He fell forward and grabbed hold of the corner rail.

"Stop throwing stuff at me!" Eddie yelled.

It felt like the men were throwing dirt and even small rocks. Eddie yanked a handkerchief out of the pocket of his jeans and desperately wiped his glasses trying to dislodge the black. The dirt spray was steady now and it felt warm.

Eddie looked up from the handkerchief. An orange glow was emanating from the ground below. With a start, Eddie realized that this was not the work of his fellow construction workers. This was too elaborate a prank for them. The platform on which he knelt began to shake once more. Eddie clung to the pieces of wood around him, desperately trying to avoid tipping over the edge and plunging into the darkness.

"God help me," he breathed.

··◆ ◆ ◆ ◆··

Ian walked to the center of a cluster of cubicles, stopping once he reached a desk with a name plate that read, "Takki, Programmer." He slammed down a box—half filled with cold pizza—on top of a stack of papers.

"Where you been, Ian?" a voice called out from over the top of one of the cubicle walls.

"I've been communicating with Neptons by way of wireless broadband," Ian replied as he grabbed a soft drink out of the mini-refrigerator he kept underneath his desk. "What do you care? Are you planning to rat me out to Pinell?"

"I don't need to. … He's been looking for you for the past three hours. And, by the way, the Neptons don't use broadband—they have mind-flow… which you would know if you paid attention."

"Yeah, well pay attention to this," Ian said as he stood up to drape one arm over the top of the cubicle wall.

"Real nice, Ian, real original. I bet you don't know what that hand signal means in the Seventh Sector."

"You've been to the Seventh Sector? I don't believe it."

"Yeah, I got there last night. I only had to hack like a quadrillion memory pendants but I've got this awesome virtual mansion now. And my virtual wife—she's hot."

"Really," Ian said, genuinely impressed. "Email me a picture."

"Done, like an hour ago."

"Let me check it out."

Ian flipped on his monitor. He minimized a screen filled with code and opened up his email. He scrolled through about fifty new messages that showed up in bold.

"My psycho girlfriend kept me up all night talking about some paper she's writing. I haven't been able to play video games for the past month. … Yeah, here it is—I got your picture. Whoah! I've got to get out of the Binid Island lair—I'm going to use this as my screen saver …"

Ian stopped and jumped as he felt someone tapping on his shoulder. He turned to see a small bespectacled man angrily trying to look over him and at his computer screen.

"Pinell—where have you been?" Ian called out a little too quickly. "I've been looking all over for you—Boyd will vouch for me."

The voice came back from over the cubicle wall, "I will not! I think you ought to fire him!"

"I'll handle this, Boyd," Pinell said.

He grabbed a broken chair from out in the hall and pulled it into the cubicle. He intertwined the fingers on his hands behind his balding head and leaned back. In doing so, he nearly fell over as the broken back to the chair gave way. He managed to catch his balance by leaning up against the fuzzy wall of the cubicle.

"We need to talk, Ian."

"I'd love to, but I'm awfully busy right now," Ian said as he turned back to face the computer screen. "This is company time, you know."

Pinell continued to speak in the direction of the broad back of Ian's head. All he could see was the thick black hair where it met up with the stained off-white collar of Ian's shirt.

"Show me what you're working on."

"You see it right here. I've been putting this code together for hours now. Look, my if-then statements are all indented… See how pretty they look when I scroll down."

Ian's thick neck prevented Pinell from seeing most of the screen. Pinell stood up and leaned over so he could take a closer look at the monitor. He grabbed his glasses by the wire rims to push them toward his eyes.

"How do I know you've done anything at all since yesterday? Have you been putting in the comments as I asked?"

"I told you—I indented all of my if-then statements. That was like a ton of work…"

"That's a five-minute macro, and you know it. I'm not as dumb as you think I am."

"I don't think you're dumb. It sounds like you have a self-esteem issue going on…"

Angrily, Pinell turned to face Ian. His face was about five inches from Ian's hooked nose.

"What I have is an 'Ian problem!' I can't get him to do simple tasks that I ask, and I can't even get him to work the hours that he's scheduled for."

"Hey, let's all relax here. There's no reason to get personal. Why don't you have a breath mint, sit down, and get calm?" Ian said, as he pulled open the top drawer of his desk and pulled a pack of gum from out of the clutter. He pulled out a stick, unwrapped it, and popped it into his large mouth. Pinell, in the meantime, walked to the other side of Ian and grabbed for his mouse.

"Hey!" Ian exclaimed, putting his large palm on top of Pinell's hand. "This is my personal equipment."

"This is NOT your personal equipment! This is a company computer. Now show me what you've got minimized there."

"What do you mean?" Ian asked, taking control of the mouse again as Pinell pulled his hand away.

"Down there—that file you've got minimized on your task bar. Click on it!"

Ian reluctantly did as he was told. A large, colorful picture of a bikini-clad woman filled the screen.

"That's just Boyd's wife—his virtual wife. He sent it to me…" Ian turned to face the cubicle wall. "What's your problem, Boyd—why are you sending me this crap? It's a waste of company resources…"

"You told me to send it!" a voice replied.

"Boyd, enough! I'll deal with you later," Pinell called over the wall. He then turned back to face down Ian, "This just isn't working out … again."

"You mean because of this? It's just pixels, dots of light, when you think about it. It only looks like a hot chick because you've got a dirty mind. … What, you're going to fire me?"

"Yes, I might have to fire you…"

"And then you'll be forced to hire me back in a month or two. We've been through this all before—you needed me back for the spring rush and then again when the Boucher program went down…"

"That Boucher program went down because you made a buggy program. I've already told the partners I'm not hiring you back to fix any more of your own programs. You just keep putting errors into your programs because you think we'll keep hiring you to fix them…"

"Well, there's the fall rush—and who's going to communicate with Boyd? He doesn't exactly speak English…"

"This isn't a joke. You think I don't know what it's like around here. I used to be a programmer before they made me department head."

"Yeah, like they need COBOL back around here."

"I'm not talking about me programming again. I'm talking about the fact that you could clean up your act and become something with this company ... we could use an assistant scheduler ..."

"Yeah, like that's going to happen. We've got so many old people around here with seniority—why don't you baby boomers just die already!"

"Obviously, I'm not ..."

"The server just went down!" the voice from over the wall called out.

"Well, Boyd, then call IT. I'm kind of tied up over here!" Pinell yelled back.

The lights went out. The humming of computers and clacking of keys ceased. The building became dead silent. The silence broke when Ian called out, "Hey? Anyone wanna play hide and seek?"

··✦✦✦✦··

I wish this place would just wash away, Sal Caretz thought as he pulled his Toyota Echo out of the driveway of his 2-story ranch-styled home and steered it down the street and past other ranch-styled homes nearly identical to the one he owned with his wife. *If she didn't always go on about her home improvement projects, maybe I wouldn't spend so many hours at the school on my days off.*

Aside from that thought, here is Caretz' collected wit and wisdom, the cream of the crop of thoughts that occurred to him as he drove from his Vancouver, Washington home towards work:

That porch looks nice. We need something on the front of our house. I wonder if you can get some sort of vinyl, so you don't have to stain it all the time.

I wish he'd pick up the pace a little. These speed bumps aren't that big a deal if you steer towards the center.

They've to have a lawn service. I could putt on that grass.

Where does she think I'd get the money from to put in a new kitchen this year?

That girl at the bus stop—she's pretty hot. I wish Carenna had red hair like that. I wonder if that chick has got red hair down …

Son of a bitch! Why don't you use your signal next time?! Ass wipe…

I don't like the PT Cruiser. It looks too much like a Hearst, from the back—or one of those old bread vans.

Damn cops. Why are they always out on afternoons like this—when the tax-paying citizens are out driving? Why don't they come out at night or go after the real problem drivers—like that guy back there? I hope you get eye cancer from that thing. I hate cops.

Am I going to hit every light today? Just my luck, the bridge will be up going over the Columbia.

Mother fucker! Golly! Did you not see me trying to get in? What, do I have to signal every time I'm gonna make a lane change for you people to pay attention?

Sal maneuvered into the traffic heading south, on I-5, toward Portland, Oregon. As he drove, as he left the suburbs of Vancouver and entered the big city, he changed. The change was noticeable from the moment he left his driveway but it became all the more pronounced as he crossed over the Columbia River on the bridge. He became a man that would be difficult for his wife to recognize, one that wouldn't fit into the neighborhood association or do well at the golf club. As he crossed the bridge, he became entirely controlled by his reptilian brain. He was competitive, unwilling to let any other car pass his own. He was territorial, daring any other car to cut into his lane.

He would punish violators of his rules with a loud blast from his horn and by screaming or giving them the one-finger wave. In a worst-case scenario, he would chase them down and cut them off to pay them back for having done the same to him. If he had to kill everyone on the highway—himself included—to make sure that his justice had been served, then so be it. His was the law of the claw.

Nor did this unbridled display of id end once he had exited the freeway and entered the streets surrounding his place of work in downtown Portland. The more anonymous he became amidst the traffic and the crowds, the more base the expression of his urges.

As he drove by, he openly ogled the women out for walks on summer afternoons, making no pretense at anything other than his base sexual desire. He could feel the blood pulse through him as female shapes floated past his windshield in an array of colors and sizes.

He hunted parking spaces with abandon. He gunned his engine and shot down city streets in search of this prey.

He reveled in the smells of food as he walked out of his parking garage and past Pioneer Square. He drank in the music played on the street corners. He confronted the protestors who carried signs and dared them to walk in his path.

He turned up his nose as he passed a teenager with the nose ring who had her arms wrapped around her knees—who begged for change near the front doors of his place of work,

Herald Junior College. Sal didn't even bother to give her a full glance as he walked past in stony silence. He knew she just would just use the money for drugs or booze.

These people, controlled by their lusts and emotions, always ending up on the wrong side of the law, Sal Caretz thought. *I don't understand them.*

As he went through the doors, the change in Sal Caretz completed once more. There he became the mild-mannered bespectacled professor who wore a sweater vest. There he became Mr. Caretz. He became the coworker who politely addressed the receptionist at the front desk. He invented idle chit-chat as his messages and student papers were retrieved. He approached students with a cheerful, "Good afternoon! It's great to see you," as he passed them in the hallway. He greeted faculty members with his Friday greeting, "I do so love teaching—it'd be perfect if it weren't for the students," as he entered the faculty lounge.

He exchanged gossip about other faculty members—who was on the wagon, who was off, who was being investigated for sexual harassment, who was having an affair, and then emailed his hearty and enthusiastic approval of the latest initiatives to the dean. He then whined about these same initiatives to his coworkers until the college president strolled down to the coffee maker—at which time he offered to fetch the coffee for her and congratulated her on having chosen such a fine dean who was producing such fine initiatives.

He then walked down the hallway and tried to remember who he was before he became a teacher. There had been another Sal Caretz, before he entered the classroom, but that model didn't work here. He had quickly learned that you can't yell at students when they pass notes, fail to pay attention, or ask stupid questions—otherwise, you would spend all of your time yelling. You also can't hit them. You certainly can't let them call you by your first name. You can't smile until at least the second week of the term, and then only when you're belittling the abilities of one of them. You can't ever be in a room, with a closed door, alone with a student—male or female. You can't show favoritism. You can't let down your guard for even a moment. You must always remember that they are students; they are not colleagues and are certainly not your friends. The one that tells you how great you are (and how lousy all of the others are) is saying the same thing to each of the other teachers behind your back.

Sal wondered if it was any different at the university, or if teaching everywhere was all the same. In any case, he would never have a definitive answer to the question since he didn't hold a doctorate. He was forever forbidden to enter the hallowed halls of Oregon's Portland University, just up the road, because of his lack of credentials.

In education, you are always judged by the degrees you hold, just as you judge the worthiness of others by their degrees. Doctorates simply don't associate with masters, who in turn won't hold court with baccalaureates. Ivy Leaguers beat out state college faculty every time. The western style of education has produced the finest caste system that has ever been known.

When Sal took classes at the university, he meekly completed the assignments asked of him by his superiors, his professors. Now as a college professor, he complied with every edict passed down by the president and deans; his objections never amounted to anything more than idle complaints in the faculty room which he would have denied if called before the faculty senate. In turn, he expected the same sort of compliance from his students, since he held sway over their access to a degree. This is the sort of compliance that has always been present in education. It's the only way the system works. This, of course, is the same system that prides itself on producing independent thinkers.

There were no urges that Sal Caretz had to hold more in check in the classroom than those of a sexual nature. College professors are priests who haven't taken vows. Sal had never done anything sexually inappropriate with any student. What he didn't know was if that was because he was filled with integrity or because no one had ever offered. Sal was a relic in a world given over to the young and sexually attractive. Every year, as he grew older, the students grew younger and prettier. It was as if they had found a fountain of youth that was denied to him.

There was a whole world inhabited by these young bodies which he was forced to ignore. When the students discussed MTV icons they wanted to see naked, sexual affairs, and wild parties (where orgies seemed to break out around every corner), he pretended not to hear. When they wore the latest fashions in clothing (or lack thereof), he pretended not to see the tattooed breasts or flat stomachs with pierced belly buttons.

Sal had gone through sexual harassment training, so he fully understood the expectations in regards to quid pro quo requests for sex and the proper language to use to avoid making students of any gender (male, female, or transgendered) feel in any way uncomfortable. He had even gone through training on the proper angle from which to approach seated female students so they wouldn't feel as if he was looking down their blouses (from the side or the back—never the front).

When Sal Caretz, from his office window, saw Anna Frod in the student courtyard, he remembered the tightly folded essay he had shoved into the front pocket of his pants. Without thinking about it, he ducked out to the patio to see her. And, since she was sitting, he made sure he approached her from the back.

"Good afternoon, Ms. Frod," he said, and then stopped to clear his throat. "I thought I saw you down here. The receptionist just handed me your paper and I was about to go over it. Let's see what it says here…"

As he fumbled with his glasses and pulled the essay out of his pocket, Caretz realized the training was wrong. He could still see down the front of Anna's gray sweat jacket, even from this angle. He was suddenly very aware of the fact that Anna wasn't wearing a bra. Her pear-shaped breasts were only as far away as the zipper on her sweat jacket.

…I could rip open her sweatshirt—break the zipper right off! Then I'd start licking her tits. I would work my tongue down across her flat stomach and towards her … Did she see me looking at her chest? Sal wondered as he turned to the side.

He nervously tossed her paper onto the table beside where she sat. He felt as if Anna was staring right through him as he made small talk. He continued to talk, but she didn't respond. She just seemed to be staring up at him, intently.

Is she interested in me? Sal mused. *Is she coming onto me?*

Sal was suddenly aware that he was sweating around the eyes. His glasses seemed to be misting up, and his vision became blurred.

"Let's see," he tried to sound confident as he ran his hand through his hair to keep it out of his eyes and turned to read Anna's paper. "… A B+ student … have decided to…"

Caretz looked up in alarm. His words came out in bursts.

"You've decided to kill yourself! Because of my class! No, no, I'm up for review! How long have you been awake? I've got to get you some sleeping pills—I've got a bottle in my office. We'll just pour a bunch of those into you and everything…"

Sal wondered if he was having a heart attack. He was suddenly warm. His collar felt too tight, and he was sweating like a pig. Blackness began to swirl all around. It was thicker than fog and seemed to consist of a fine black powder. Sal became aware of the fact that this was happening outside of his own body.

Suddenly, the entire building began to shake and there was a shriek let loose by a student who sat in the corner behind where Sal and Anna were positioned. The glass table tipped over and the surface shattered against the cement deck. As the shaking subsided, a large group of students and staff came running out into the mid-afternoon darkness. Excitedly they rushed toward the edge of the patio, almost with glee. Black flakes, like some sort of otherworldly snow-fall, dropped on the group.

"What's going on?" Sal asked as he and Anna rushed up to the group at the edge.

"It's a huge chain of volcanic explosions! The electricity has gone down in there, but I'm picking it up on my portable radio," a young woman with a headphone jammed against her ear said. "I've been trying to get Internet access up on my cell phone, but the cellular network seems to have gone down."

Soon everyone was asking questions at once. Since there wasn't much to see in the darkness, they tried to fill in the picture with the hints given on the girl's ancient AM dial.

"Volcanic explosions—where?"

"Everywhere—all along the Pacific Coast—throughout the West! Mt. Shasta, Mt. Adams, Rainier, Hood, St. Helens—it all happened without warning. They're saying it's all happening without showing up first on their seismographs! They don't know what to expect…"

"Are there people hurt?"

"Yes!" the woman said excitedly. "Lots of them, who knows how many … they say they'll be recovering the dead for weeks, maybe months or years! It wiped out Vancouver!"

"Vancouver," one man repeated. "But my partner and I go there all of the time—it's so open and welcoming to all lifestyles…"

"Not that Vancouver … not B.C. … Just north of us … the Vancouver in Washington!"

"There's a Vancouver in Washington?" the man asked. "Are you sure?"

"Yes," Sal said, quietly. "That's where I live."

Anna turned to face her professor. He looked as if he had just had all of the life sucked out of him as he stood slumped against a cement planter that stood atop the edge of the balcony, with black soot falling upon him. She realized that he must have lost everything. She vaguely recalled that he had a wife—it seemed a strange thought to think of her professor as someone who could be romantically involved, who could love and be loved. As Anna thought of this, she felt within herself the deep pain that he must be feeling at the loss of his wife.

What do you do in a situation like this, when someone has lost everything? Anna wondered. *What is the appropriate response?*

Anna put her hand on his shoulder. She awkwardly pulled herself towards Mr. Caretz and hugged him.

If Vancouver was gone, Sal realized that he had probably lost everything. His house, his other car, his suits and ties, his golf clubs ... the list seemed endless. Then Sal felt Anna's arm on his shoulder, and her breast rubbing against his forearm as she hugged him. He wondered if she was coming onto him and once again was thankful that he knew the difference between appropriate and inappropriate behavior—even if others lost their heads at a time like this.

The woman with the radio pulled the headphone away from her ear and said, "The radio just went out—I can't get in any station, AM or FM."

"What did they say?" someone cried out. "What was the last thing they said?"

"They said something much worse is on the way."

II - Boy Meets Girl

The Columbia River is fed by rivers that originate in Idaho to the east and Canada to the north. It extends all of the way to the edge of the West Coast and to the Pacific Ocean. It comprises the largest portion of the border between Oregon and Washington. Before those states existed, it separated British territory from that claimed by the Americans. It was the main source of inland fish for the Indians who lived in the region long before anyone was around to call them Indians. The fish owned it before that, the bacteria before that, and the U.S. Corps of Army Engineers created it (that last part might not be exactly true, but they sure act like it).

There are two routes through Portland that take you north. The first is the Glenn Jackson Bridge, which has a nice view of Mt. Hood on clear days, and an icy pavement on cold days; it winds east towards Camas before heading north through Orchards (where there are no orchards, only track housing), Battle Ground (where some battle might have once taken place, but no one knows for sure, as it has all been covered in track housing), and Salmon Creek (where there are no creeks and, most likely as a result, no salmon, and where—as a change of pace—it has all been covered in track housing). At this point, the highway (205) meets up with I-5.

Interstate 5 makes no pretense of any sort; it just heads straight through downtown Vancouver (which died when they created the mall and the track housing—but the mayor still clings to the belief that people might one day spurn the suburbs for an inner-city teeming with drug addicts, if only he convinces the taxpayers to build it) and gets you to Seattle as quickly as possible. Along the way, it bypasses as many majestic wonders as possible—including the Puget Sound, Mt. Rainier, and Mt. Hood. If you go south on this highway you can get to California, but no one has ever figured out a sane reason for doing such a thing.

Californians keep following this highway north, however, which is why home prices skyrocketed in the Portland/Vancouver metro area, and which is also why people keep building homes (most of which look like everyone else's home) as they spread north through former farming towns, like Ridgefield and La Center.

This sprawl has moved people looking for wilderness even farther north, to communities like Cougar and Woodland which lie near the base of Mt. St. Helens. This is an active volcano, which might make you wonder why anyone would live near it. The answer is probably that people have a desire to live in harmony with nature even when nature does not wish to live in harmony with them. Yet there people live, trapped between a volcanic mountain and a tremendous river. Many of these same people marvel at the fact that Romans once lived on the isle of Pompeii, trapped between a mighty volcano and the sea. Mountains do, from time to time, awaken to unleash their fury. This is what Mt. St. Helens decided to do—at precisely the same time as nearly every other mountain on the West Coast.

It didn't give any warning to the scientists at the observation point. The chief geologist was standing at a window overlooking the dome of the mountain when it erupted. She was telling one of her colleagues a joke, "Do you know what the last thing is to go through a gnat's head when it hits your car's windshield?" she asked and then answered, "Its feet." Those were her last words. A blast with the same power as a nuclear explosion ripped through the window directly in front of where she was standing.

Farther away, a farmer at the northern edge of La Center sensed something as he looked off in the distance from his back porch. He stopped, bent forward, placed his head between his legs, held tight to his knees with his elbows, and strained to push his head upward, behind himself. From the kitchen window overlooking this scene stood his wife, Vera. Presently she decided to question him, "Merle, you've done some mighty strange things in your life, but this is downright the most peculiar. What in tarnation are you doing?"

"Why, Vera," Merle replied, as he continued to strain to move his head upward from his bent-over position, "I am trying mightily to kiss my ass goodbye."

Less than a split second later, a 20-foot-high flow of lava rolled over Merle and Vera. They were forever preserved in place.

In a classroom just down the road, a young student was at the window. He yelled out, "Teacher, teacher, my super vision tells me that something big is headed this way."

"Dallas, you don't have super vision. We are all equal in this classroom; therefore we are all special," she said, as she gestured toward the group of children gathered around her. "Come, join us in the special circle."

Dallas did as he was told. He took a seat on the floor amidst a ring of children who all sat with folded legs. "Now, children, we're beginning to hear news reports of some sort of minor eruption up on Mt. St. Helens. What I want you to know is that there is nothing to fear but fear itself. You are safe right here in your school."

At that very moment, the wave of lava rolled through the school building, that final lesson permanently memorialized.

A man in Battle Ground drove home from his job in Portland to have lunch with his wife. He came through the front door of the house bearing flowers. "I'm home dear—just like you've always asked. I drove from Portland to Vancouver just to have lunch with you," he called out as he headed through the house in search of his wife. "Let me tell you, the traffic is murder. There's some sort of fog rolling in and …" Just then, he opened the door to the next room. He stopped mid-sentence. "Sheila, I can't believe it! In our own house … and you, Jane, … Just what do you think you two're doing?" Whatever the answer was it was drowned out by the wave of lava and mud that tore through the home, and whatever happened there in Battle Ground that day will forever stay buried in Battle Ground.

In an old folk's home in Orchards, a nurse was pushing an elderly gentleman in his wheelchair through the garden. She looked off in the distance and saw the furl of black heading directly for them and behind that what appeared to be a ring of fire. She screamed and took off running.

The old man woke up from his nap and saw what had caused his nurse to scream. He frantically tried to push his wheelchair out of harm's way, as he was being pelted by ash and falling debris, and he quickly realized it was of no use. On trembling legs, he stood to his feet. Gingerly, he took a step. Finding that he could do this, he took another. "I can walk! I can walk!" he yelled in delight, just as the wave of fire hit.

At center stage in the empty Five Corners Heritage auditorium, a young woman sat down at a black grand piano and began to play Mozart's 71st Symphony rhythmically, her long dark fingers alternating between the white and black keys as the lava poured all around her.

A bare-footed old man carried his three-year-old granddaughter through the blackness as he ran to the south, the flow of lava was almost upon them. The little girl saw it about to hit them from her perch atop her grandfather's shoulder. "I'm scared!" she cried. "Don't be scared. I'll save you!" he barked back. He pulled her down from his shoulders and pushed her head against his chest as the first wave of lava nipped at his heels. He wrapped her up tight in his arms as the pain seared through the soles of his feet. Momentarily, the swell broke over them both.

An old woman and man lay together in bed as the darkness closed in from every pore in their home. She looked at him and smiled. He took her hand and placed it on his heart. It busted at the very same moment that the lava burst through their bedroom wall.

Outside a car was swept along in the currents of the lava. A house bobbed along behind it, chasing it, until both were consumed by flames and descended into the depths of the liquid.

"What's that?" a blind woman asked, as her dog began to yip at her. "We need to get out of here! It's an emergency! Oh, yes, good dog. Let me just get ready …" She walked over to her wall and felt along it for the bottom edge of a picture frame. She lifted the picture off of the wall and felt along the space until she found the ridged plastic knob. The dog growled at her, as she slowly twisted in the combination and opened the safe. It tried to tug at her dress with its teeth as she began to pull the contents loose. "Just a second … I need this!" she said, slapping at the dog just as they were both permanently submerged under the molten swell.

A man stuck in traffic on I-5, just a hundred yards north of the bridge over the Columbia River, sensed that something was wrong as a thick black haze filled the air. He got out of his car, put his head down, and ran. He sprinted onto the bridge and raced past everyone, only to stop—out of breath—when he reached a group of people in the middle of the span, where they were all staring back up the highway in stunned silence. The man looked back and saw lava pouring into the Columbia River at the foot of the bridge and all along the bank. Where he had been running, just seconds before, was now completely covered in a thin but steady sheet of the fiery liquid.

Back in the lava flow, he saw people whose feet and legs had become completely immersed, toppling lifeless. Cars were being carried along, slowly sparking and burning as they moved. He saw a woman clinging to the top of her BMW despite the raging heat. Then the car banged against a telephone pole; it flipped over and the woman was erased. All that was left was her scream. The screams echoed. It was then that the man realized that the group he was standing with was screaming also. And he too was screaming as the super-heated metal at the base of the bridge gave way.

The entire group was pitched forward and downward, towards the broiling waters far below. As the man screamed, he fell. As he fell, he held out his arms, hoping for something to grab.

·· + + ◆ + +··

How many people have died? We'll have an updated death count for you in less than five minutes. Remember, stick with us here for 'News that is To the Point' all day and evening long—we're the station with more death totals than any other here in Portland…

"I think the drain is clogged up—I was covered in ash," Anna said as she walked out of the apartment's bathroom and into the living room with a towel covering her hair. "What's the latest total?" She zipped up her gray hooded jacket as she walked over to an oversized bean bag in the center of the room. There her boyfriend sat holding a remote control and a tub of popcorn watching the news on their 32-inch plasma flat-screen TV. "Dunno. They just keep running the same stories over and over," Ian replied, his mouth full of popcorn. Salted and buttered popcorn crumbs clung to the sides of his chin, flipping through the stations as he spoke.

Anna tossed the towel aside and, since there wasn't room on the bean bag for her, lay down on the dirty laminate wood floor beside him. Ian's thick body had driven a deep furrow into the chair and the foam beans had all been displaced to the sides of the black vinyl bag. Anna kicked off her tennis shoes. "Hold up," she said. "Go back—to channel 8. I think I saw something. ..." She stopped speaking as the news anchor made his announcements. She strained to hear over the top of Ian's smacking lips.

We're going live now to the edge of what used to be I-5 north. Our 'First on the Scene' reporter, Joan Acadia, is talking to a survivor of the bridge's collapse. ... Hold on, it appears we're having some sort of technical difficulty—that's footage from an old episode of 'Hee Haw.' ... OK, now I'm being told that Joan is on. Joan, can you hear me?

Yes, John, this is Joan Acadia reporting live from Jantzen Beach where rescuers have set up a makeshift shelter in the middle of the shopping center for displaced residents. I'm standing here with ...

"I already saw this guy on Channel Two," Ian said as he lifted the remote so he could change channels.

Anna reached up and pushed the remote back down, "Wait—I was stuck in downtown for three hours until the electricity came back on and they got the MAX up and running again. I haven't seen any of this."

"It wasn't like it was easy for me to get back here either, you know ..."

...That's right, Joan, I held onto the railing for nearly an hour, until the rescue helicopter came and got me. I had sea gulls picking at my head and arms the entire time—that's why I've got all these cuts and bruises. I still don't know how I managed to grab hold of anything ... I was just falling ...

Well, Ed, that is an amazing story. They're telling me that footage is running of that helicopter rescue on screen for our viewers at home. That, of course, is another advantage of our 'First on the Scene' coverage of V Day. Now, tell me, when you first went running for the bridge, what kept you going as so many people around you were falling into the lava?

I've got'ta say, it's like this: I already knew what was behind me, so I just kept moving forward.

"That's a cheesy line… you want some popcorn?"

"No … quiet …"

…So that's what I've got from here. Live from Jantzen Beach, with our exclusive 'First on the Scene' coverage, I'm Joan Acadia.

Thanks, Joan. Of course, I'm John Stassel, and we are well into hour three of our 'First on the Scene' coverage of what we've been calling V Day. Again, for anyone who is just now waking up from a coma, this is V or Volcano Day. A day we'll all remember for the rest of our lives… a day when at least 10 volcanoes erupted all along the Pacific Coast, most in a minor way, with the exception of Mt. St. Helens which is now nothing more than a large hole in the ground. We now know that it erupted at 3:11 this afternoon—without warning—discharging boulders, debris, and a huge wave of lava. Thousands, perhaps hundreds of thousands, of people have died—stay tuned; we'll have more on that count in a few minutes. Many of the dead are just up north of us, where the towns of Cougar, Woodland, Ridgefield, La Center, Battle Ground, and Vancouver all vanished within minutes. It is a day when portions of two major highways, I-5 and 205, have been destroyed. The Columbia River has risen to dangerous levels as lava has been pouring into it for the past three hours. And we still don't know much about the condition of Camas… we're only now beginning to get sketchy reports that …

"Boring," Ian said with a sigh, as he lifted his body up and out of the bean bag—which responded with a sigh of its own, "I'm going to see if the bloggers have any better news. I'll be in the bedroom—your laptop is in there, right?"

"Yes, yes, fine … I'm trying to listen," Anna said. She started to move into the bean bag but decided against it when she felt the top of it with her hand. Ian had left the vinyl surface wet from perspiration and slick from his buttery fingers.

...as you can see from these shots, the landscape will never be the same. You have to strain to see it, because of all of the ash in the air, but these are preliminary pictures from some of the biggest mountains in the Cascade Range. There's a view of Mt. Lassen, Shasta, Baker ... OK, let's see, is this Glacier Peak? I'm being told that is exactly what it is. Of course, that's Mt. Rainier, which sustained only minor damage as you can see, much to the relief of our neighbors to the north in Seattle. ... There's Adams, and that, folks, believe it or not, is what is left of Mt. St. Helens.

"Can you get me a beer?" Ian called out from the bedroom.

"No, get it yourself!" Anna called back, fidgeting angrily with the zipper on her hooded sweatshirt as she mumbled, "This is exactly why I'm killing myself..."

Ian, who was crossing behind her to get to the refrigerator, said, "So you're still doing that? I told you it won't work... you'll fall into a coma first. How long has it been?"

Anna flipped her body over, lying with her stomach on the floor, so she could see her boyfriend. Ian, in the meantime, held a can in his large hands and was popping it open.

"Over 27 hours now. You aren't going to have me around much longer. Another 189 hours..."

"Yeah, ... whatever... You'll never make it. You always start these things and never finish them."

"You just don't believe in me," Anna said, flipping back over from her stomach to her back and lifting her skinny legs into the air to stretch them. "Trust me; I'm going to go all the way this time."

"Well, you might not have to worry about it anyway," Ian said, as he crossed back through the living room and into the bedroom behind her. "It looks like they're about to cover it on the news there, but the blogs are going wild with the story already..."

Anna was already watching the news being broken on the television screen. Beneath John Stassel, between the "First on the Scene" logo and a freshly-prepared "V-Day" logo, a red marquee—with white lettering—announced "Breaking News."

...and again, this is just now being reported nationally. Let's go live now to our anchor desk in New York, where William Hert is already covering this live...

...the statement is expected to be made in about 20 minutes, around 9:40 Eastern Standard time. I'm being told now that our network affiliates all along the Pacific are just now joining us, so let me bring everyone up to speed. I'm William Hert. As most of you already know a series of volcanoes—at least 10 eruptions—occurred without warning earlier this afternoon, at about 6:11 pm. More importantly, the result for us here on the East Coast is that we'll experience a series of disruptive weather events and it is likely that the entire Eastern Seaboard will be swamped by an echo tsunami of Biblical proportions. We're now learning that this is almost certainly not an isolated event. The President of the United States, using information supplied to him by the United States Department of Science Service, headed by Dr. Oppenheimer Ulent, is going to announce that this is just the beginning of a much larger series of eruptions that is about to devastate the entire Pacific Coast. An aide to the president, who spoke with one of our White House reporters anonymously, is saying that they believe this series of eruptions will be powerful enough to sever the entire West Coast from the North American continent. This will set in motion a chain of events that will wreak havoc all across the Northern hemisphere, including Europe and the Middle East. In short, the President is prepared

to announce the onset of a cataclysmic event that is likely to end civilization as we know it.

We'll carry that live in about 20 minutes. Those of you expecting to see the Sweet 16 tournament will need to watch it on our sister cable network ...

"Did you hear what they said? The world is about to end, " Anna said as she covered up her tiny mouth with both of her hands, sucked in a breath, and then uncovered her mouth to continue, "Look up this Dr. Ulent, will you? I think I've heard that name somewhere before."

"What do you think I've been doing? ... Just give me a second ..."

Well, a lot is happening nationally, and we'll break back into our local coverage as soon as the President begins speaking. In the meantime, we've got another viewer poll question up for you. The question is this: Should we go on calling this V-Day, or should we change it to EW-Day—EW for the end of the world? The phone call costs .55 cents and you dial into the number listed on your screen. There's an additional charge for text messages. This is the only station where, 'You Vote, You Decide.'

Now we've got the harrowing story of a cat that survived atop a rock out in the middle of the lava for over 2 hours...

"Alright, I've got some stuff," Ian called out from the bedroom. "This Ulent heads up the U.S. Department of Science, in D.C., but he has a second home..."

"I know that."

"I know you know that, I heard the news too. ... But, like I was going to say, he still has a house right around here, down in Lake Oswego. He's been here in town for the past year because he was overseeing the manned mission into Mt.

St. Helens that went up in smoke last month…" Ian's voice cracked, and he stopped to clear it.

"That's the one where they sent in the probe filled with scientists and the thing exploded, right?" Anna called back.

"Yeah, something like that. All of the scientists died. The blogs say it looked like Ulent was going to be forced to resign when the final congressional report came back—that was the rumor in Washington for the past couple of weeks. Oh wait, I've got something good here…"

Anna heard the keys clacking away in the bedroom. Ian hummed, let out a low whistle, and then cursed.

"What is it?"

"Well, just now I cracked into some sort of secret government file—it was just floating around, they had left a trapdoor open; the feds are idiots. … Anyway, I found some sort of report that listed Ulent's home address in Oswego. I had a birth date. I even had some sort of top-secret report…"

"What did that say?"

"I'm getting to that. Well, I just saw the heading: '51 Ways To End Your World.' But before I could look at it, the security kicked in and a cyber root entangled me. I think I managed to get his birth date and home address copied in a temp file."

"Isn't this exciting? The world is going to end, isn't it? It's finally happening—something big is finally going to happen to us!" Anna said as she stood up in the living room, her bony knees cracking from the pressure of standing after such a long time of lying down. She then quietly walked over to stand in the bedroom doorway. There she looked in at Ian, who was furiously typing away on the keyboard. He was facing in her direction—the laptop turned away from the doorway. He sat on the edge of their queen-sized bed. He was so engrossed in the screen that he didn't even notice her standing there. Anna had become used to his way of ignoring her like this.

As she stood there, she wondered what she had ever seen in him. Ian had dark, shaggy hair that looked like it had been cut using sheep shears. His eyes had epicanthic folds. He had a hooked nose and overly square jaw. His face was wide and constantly covered with the crumbs of whatever meal he had last eaten. He always wore shorts with a draw string and a t-shirt around the apartment, just like he wore now. This revealed his thick and hairy arms and legs. His toes were buried in the bedroom's deep shag carpet, except for his unkempt and dirty toenails which stuck out above the surface like talons.

Yet as she watched him, Anna remembered exactly why she had fallen for him in the first place. Ian was a cocky smart ass who didn't care what anyone else thought of him. He was so sure of himself, just as she always doubted herself. Thinking back, Anna felt a tingle of excitement as she remembered how they had met. Ian had stepped in and cursed out some bus driver who hadn't stopped to let her off at the corner of Glisan and 10th. He might well be a jerk, but it was nice to have a jerk on your side. See, everyone needs to jerk off now and then.

As Anna sat there and watched Ian, she realized that he might be the last man she would ever have the chance to be with, seeing as how the world was about to end and she was in the middle of committing suicide and all. Ian, for his part, had bored of researching Ulent and had switched over to looking at Internet porn. He was straining to see a low-resolution movie that purportedly showed two real-life sorority girls gone wild. He didn't like the scripted stuff.

Is that a nipple? he thought. *No, that's not a nipple… hey, wait a second—this looks like two guys in drag…*

His slutty-sorority research was interrupted by Anna's voice, as she called out, "Hey, come help me out here… I need some help with something that I've got turned on." She stood there, in the doorway, completely naked, her sweat suit and panties down around her ankles. She struck a pose that she hoped would be sexy, with her arms lifted up and elbows spread out so as to pull her small breasts into an uplifted position, her nipples puffy and dark red. She ran a hand through the short dark hairs on the back of her head and ran her tongue over the fingers of her other hand, as she passed it in front of her lip-stick-free mouth.

Ian never saw the show that she was putting on. He never looked up. Flushed with the surprise of her standing there, he was too busy trying to close out all of the pop-up porn ad screens so she wouldn't see them. Desperately he clicked around trying to open some of the Ulent files.

"I wouldn't worry about this end of the world thing," he said, a little too assuredly. "The blogs here say that if anyone can save this world, this Ulent man can do it. They say that he's some sort of ex-KGB genius who defected from the Ukraine." He looked up just in time to see Anna in the doorway, zipping back up the front of her sweat shirt. He looked to her for some approval. "Isn't that good news?"

"No, it isn't." Anna replied curtly. "I hope this world ends. I hope we all die. But, mostly, I want to see you gone. I'm leaving you."

"You can't leave me now," Ian said; but he thought that, if she did leave, he could probably still find those pictures he had just been looking at on the Web. "Where would you even go?"

"I know exactly where I'm going," Anna replied as she grabbed her keys and put them in the front pocket of her sweat suit. She opened the front door and continued, "If what the bloggers are saying is true, I'm going to find that Dr. Ulent and stop him from saving the world."

Anna stormed out of the front entrance, leaving the door open wide behind her. "Get out of my way, you Fuzzy Whatzle!" she said angrily out in the hall. Ian made his way through the apartment to shut the door. He looked out in the corridor to see who Anna had yelled at. Except for his retreating girlfriend, the hall was empty. "What a psycho!" he spluttered before he hurried back to his computer.

As he continued to conduct his porn research, a feeling nagged at him. Ian couldn't quite place it. It was as if he had lost something, but he couldn't remember what it was. The flow of images of young, attractive, fun-loving, sexually-active people on the screen kept him from delving too deep into such thoughts.

···◆◆◆···

Eddie opened his eyes, the pain beating through his skull as he lifted his head off of the hard surface upon which he found himself sprawled, his hard hat still in place. With his neck and head propped up by his upper arms and elbows, he tried to remember where he was and how he had gotten there. Eddie saw that the fingers of his left hand were still curled around a length of two-by-four that lay next to him on the flat top of a boulder. He felt sticky hot even though it appeared to be evening on an early spring day. To him, it felt more like the heart of summer.

Eddie tried to clear his throat, which was clogged, and tried to lick his lips only to realize they were covered in dirt or dust. He swiped the grime off the lenses of his glasses and lifted his hands to see that his palms were covered in a mixture of black liquid and thick dust. The sight of the liquid reminded him that he had been carrying a bucket of some sort before he had fallen.

Eddie groaned as he managed to roll onto his side, pain shooting through the length of his back. He pulled off his glasses with one hand and with his bare eyes, he found that the world was very dark. He squinted trying to look at the watch he wore on his right wrist and saw that it was 6:14. The last he could recall, before he had been asked to carry the bucket of tar to the top of the frame, it had been just after three.

Why would those guys just leave me lying here for three hours? he wondered. *And why is everyone so quiet?*

With his glasses off, he tried to peer through the darkness, nothing appeared to be moving. There hung a pungent smell in the air.

Over the past weeks of commuting to the work site from his parent's home in Portland, Eddie had found that Camas had a unique scent due to the giant pulp mill just outside of town. But this smell was entirely different.

As he listened, he heard some sort of movement—almost like water in a stream. He looked directly down, below the edge of the boulder on which he lay and saw a thick, heavy liquid, covered in a black crust, moving past.

Eddie then set his glasses on top of the board to one side of him. He reached down, and with his fingers extended, strained to touch the dark crust. As his fingers neared the surface, a piece of the black crust got caught on the edge of his rock, twisted, and descended. A white-orange interior bubbled into view, sparks shooting out from the golden liquid.

Eddie gasped and drew back his hand. His fingertips felt as if he had touched an oven burner. He sucked on them to draw out the heat. He was beginning to remember the orange light he had seen when he had tumbled to the corner at the top of the building frame. Even with his limited knowledge of science, he knew that this must be lava—although he had no idea how it had wound up in Camas, Washington.

Eddie mustered up some spit and used his shirt to wipe off his glasses as best as possible. He put them back on his face, where he could barely see as they were still smeared with a heavy dust. Then, as he turned to the left, he saw that the flow of black extended far off in the black distance, all along the hillside below him. In many places, the black crust was broken to reveal the boiling bright orange liquid below.

Eddie looked directly below where he was lying. He remembered seeing this rock before; in fact, the construction foreman had laid out the blueprints on it every time someone had shown up to inspect the crew's progress on the building. It was almost perfect for such a job, at a little more than four feet tall with a long, flat surface.

He wondered what exactly the rock was made of. Was it granite, or something else? It was warm, but not as hot as one would expect from a boulder surrounded by molten lava. Eddie remembered that the rock had always seemed to be of a peculiar color and texture, but he had no idea as to the sort of heat-resistant mineral that it was made of. Eddie had never paid much attention to things like this in his one geology class.

The lava was about a foot-and-a-half below from where he lay and Eddie figured from how tall the rock was previously that it was probably about two feet deep. This made some sense since the rock was just up the hill from where the building project had been taking place. This meant, Eddie realized, that the lava was probably much deeper down in the direction closer to the building footprint, where the ground had been bulldozed clear for the foundation. This also meant it was probably much less deep on the hillside higher above him. To check his math, Eddie carefully scooted towards the other side of the rock and then rolled his body back to look over that side. Sure enough, he found that the molten liquid appeared to be a few inches lower on that side. He couldn't see all the way up the hillside in the dark, but he was certain that he could see bare rock and dirt in places.

From having surveyed the construction site, Eddie knew that he was lying near the base of a big hill and that the hillside grew steeper only a few feet from where he lay. Now, he only needed to figure out exactly how many feet it was to safety.

It figures I'd wind up needing to do math. God must be trying to tell me something, Eddie thought. *Let's see, I was ok at word problems. If a man is lying on a boulder, and boiling hot lava is flowing at two feet high below that rock, while it is 8 inches high above it, how far up the hillside must a safe place be? No ... wait a second ... you'd have to figure slope in and Eldriss would have had us chart something out ... How do you calculate slope, anyway?*

Eddie lay there, looking straight up into the murky air, as he attempted to figure his way out of this situation mathematically. As he did, he forced himself to a standing position.

To hell with all of this, he thought. *Math is what got me into this mess in the first place. … Let's see, what are my assets? I'm still alive, so that means someone up there likes me. And I've got a piece of wood … hey, that's it!*

Eddie picked up the two-by-four. It was about five feet in length, with a jagged end from where it had broken off of the larger frame. That was the end that Eddie speared into the darkness, while he gripped hold of the smoothly cut end. "I'll anchor that end to the hillside, lay the board down, and walk up it," Eddie said, almost as if he was expecting someone to hear what he was saying and record it for posterity, even though no one else was around.

He felt the other end hit dirt and it looked like he might be onto something. Just when he was about to feel a sense of accomplishment, the board burst into flames. Eddie let the burning wood fall. It landed on the black crust and slowly sank as it flamed, the orange light allowing Eddie to see that there was at least a trace of the black liquid flowing as far as six feet above him, before giving way to a bare hillside.

Alright, then, genius, Eddie chided himself. *What assets do you have left? I've got my brain, which so far hasn't performed so well; I've got my good looks—short, dark, and exotic. And I've got well-developed thighs.*

So he jumped.

Whether it was because he experienced a rush of adrenalin or (as he would later claim) because he was carried by angels, Eddie managed to spring the full six feet up the hillside and land face down, with the toes of his work boots just inches above the lava.

Someday, someone will write about this, Eddie thought. *But then someone else will read about it and figure out why it's mathematically impossible for a five-foot, six-inch tall man to jump six feet up a hillside from a standing start. That's exactly why I hate math.*

Then he let his head fall towards the ash-covered ground—with the bill of his hard hat holding his face just off the surface—and he wept. Between sobs, Eddie thanked God for letting him keep his life. After a few minutes, Eddie pulled himself to his feet and scampered up the hillside. He stumbled over the top of the hill and ran towards lights he saw off in the distance. He pressed forward, knowing nothing more about what he ran towards other than that it wasn't what he had escaped at the bottom of the hill. When Eddie finally reached the lights, he nearly fell into the arms of a grizzled old man who was carrying a candle.

"Hold up there, young man," the stranger said. "Haven't we had quite enough excitement for one day?"

Eddie steadied himself with the help of the man. He looked around and saw hundreds of people were all around, all of them carrying candles. They were coming in and going out from all sorts of darkened buildings that lined the street where he now found himself.

"What is this place? What are these people doing?" Eddie asked breathlessly.

"Why, this is a church. Don't you think it's fitting to make a little time for God, what with all that is happening?"

"A church ... I've come to a church? Oh, this must be a sign from above. It's a miracle!"

"Now, hold on there, young feller. Don't get too excited," the man said. "You must be a stranger to these parts. You must not know about Camas. Why, you're standing in the city with the most churches in the entire world. We've got ourselves a church for just about everyone out here … and this here is the world-famous Camas Church Row—so it isn't that surprising that you would wind up in a church."

"It's just been a long day—I'm getting a little carried away, I guess."

"Well, try to zip it little, kid. We don't need any extra excitement. Besides, you almost sound like one of those Holy Rollers or something—miracles just don't happen to anyone anymore …" the man said, continuing to mutter as he turned and walked away—taking his light with him.

Without looking at the signs that lined the streets, Eddie followed the stream of people—most of whom carried candles—into the nearest building. Once he made his way through the anteroom and into the interior, the yellow glow from candles revealed stained glass windows and ornately carved pews. There he sat in one of the pews near the back where he had to strain to hear the leader of the group, a soft-spoken, bespectacled man in a black robe with a white collar.

Eddie remembered nothing of religion back in India, and he hadn't attended church much since the missionaries had brought his family back to America. So he wasn't familiar with the terminology or actions of the people here. They all were reading from one of the green books that had been left lying on the benches, so he opened one up and pretended to read along. When they all recited, he mumbled in tune. When they sang, he mumbled again, but off tune. When everyone else sat, Eddie sat also. Then, the speaker did something which the audience didn't expect, judging from the whispers. The black-robed man walked off of the stage and sat on one of the stairs, then he extended his long arms.

"I know that I'm breaking with tradition, but these are not traditional times. Most of you have by now heard the news from the outside world, which has slowly made its way to our little community. Over the last few hours, I've had a chance to think about it all as I prepared my message for tonight."

He folded his arms and crossed his legs. Then he continued. In direct words, he related what he had found out about the eruption of Mt. Hood and the devastation in the surrounding Southwest Washington cities.

As Eddie listened, he realized that most of the people he sat with had lost friends or family members in the destruction. Several probably didn't even know the fate of those people they loved. His own family was probably safe in Portland, but Eddie tried to imagine what it would be like to find out that your father or brother was dead.

As the black robe continued, Eddie realized that not even his own family was in the clear. He learned about the president's briefing before the nation which had taken place less than half an hour before. Judging from the gasps of the rest of the congregation, it appeared that Eddie wasn't the only one who was learning about all this for the first time. It seemed that things were worse than he could have imagined. The president had said that the release of gasses into the environment from 10 simultaneous eruptions in one day was equal to the effect of thousands of coal factories putting out carbon emissions 24 hours a day for 100 years straight. Already the result was being felt worldwide in the form of torrential rains and gathering hurricanes on the Eastern seaboard. There were blizzards made entirely of golf-ball-sized hail in the Midwest, flooding in parts of Africa and the Middle East that hadn't seen precipitation in years, and the melting polar ice caps were threatening to drown the exterior edges of several continents in weeks and months, not decades.

But that wasn't even the worst of it. Some scientist by the name of Ulent was predicting a second wave of eruptions all along the Cascade Range that would sever the West Coast from North America and drown it all in the Pacific Ocean.

As the details continued, Eddie tried to comprehend it all. He tried hard to concentrate on the essence of the message from God, if there was one. It seemed that the world was about to end—at least as far as the majority of the human population was concerned. He was amazed at how quickly his mind grasped the substance of this new reality. He was comforted to be in a place devoted to worship at this moment in time, all things considered.

"In these last few hours, maybe it's best if we discuss those things that we normally don't bring out into the open. After all, God seems to have left us to fend for ourselves; so we might as well amuse ourselves. To that end, there are many things that a priest hears in confession that he isn't allowed to repeat. But—since the world is about to end anyway—I figure, what's the harm …"

The crowd gasped. The priest just ignored it all and kept going.

"The following people have all committed one of the seven deadly sins; I'll give you a minute to guess which sin before I give you the answer. First, let's start with Ida May. Any guesses … anyone? Trust me; this will come as a shock."

An old woman stood up and grabbed hold of her walker. She yelled a specific—and somewhat unhygienic—instruction for the priest, and then slowly moved out of the room. All the while, the priest kept taking guesses from the rest of the group. More fascinated than he should have been by the angry exchanges and revelations, Eddie stayed on for a couple more minutes, before his revulsion got the better of him and he decided to leave. This was not what he had been looking for in either a church or the end of the world. As he left, the last words he heard the priest utter were, "Now for some sodomy…"

Eddie made his way down the street and into a storefront building that looked nothing like any church he had ever seen before. Inside he discovered a lively—and large—group singing to the accompaniment of a jazz band. After a spell of singing, everyone sat down on folding chairs that were haphazardly scattered around the room. Candles dripping wax lined the walls. The minister, a large black man with slicked-back hair and thick gold bands on all of his fingers, ran to the front of the room. He let out a yell as he slammed a thick Bible onto a thin, metal podium. He yanked a microphone out of a nearby stand for show—a fairly nonsensical action considering that the electricity wasn't flowing.

"Brothers and sisters, I feel a sermon coming on!" he yelled. "I've been talking to God tonight, and let me tell you, He has laid an important message upon my heart."

Eddie leaned forward expectantly. His metal chair creaked from his weight shifting. His hard hat fell forward and covered his eyes and he quickly pushed it back into place.

"God has told me that it's easier for a camel to get through the eye of a needle than it is for a rich man to make it into heaven. You might have heard people say that you can't buy your way into heaven but God told me that you had better start trying. We are standing here at the end of the world where God has told me that the rules have all changed and it's all going to be taken away! So He wants you to bring all of your earthly possessions to turn over to the church. Brothers and sisters, we are getting ready to go home to Jesus! Can I get a witness? A little louder now—let's let them hear you all the way to glory!"

The next thing Eddie knew, the entire group was in the process of piling their cash, gold bands, and jewelry into baskets. The minister was excitedly urging them to give all that they had with them.

"We are going to melt this gold into a graven image unlike any this world has ever seen. We're going to build us a Jesus statue so high that it will reach into heaven and cover it in diamonds. It will out-glory Jesus, that's how beautiful this image will be. Every knee will bow, every tongue confess that our new metal Jesus is Lord! We will be the envy of the entire world; we're going to be at the head of God's Army leading the way into the Second Coming!"

Eddie found his way out of the door. This too was not the God that had saved him that he was seeking. He sprinted desperately down the street. This time, he read the signs more carefully.

"Seventh Day Adventist ... that sounds a little like dentist—it must be professional," he said, as he went up to the church (complete with a steeple) that he found nearby and tried to open the door. The door wouldn't budge. One of the women from a group smoking nearby hailed him, "Just what do you think you're doing?"

"I'm trying to go to church. I'm trying to find God before the world ends!"

"Look, sonny, we invented the idea of the end of the world. So I can tell you with certainty that God doesn't come again until Saturday to this building!" the woman chided Eddie. "Just what sort of God are you looking for on a Friday, anyway?"

"I don't know," Eddie replied, as he turned to walk away. "A God whose name I don't know, I guess."

"Well, young man, maybe you ought to learn a bit more about the place before you try to barge into it. I don't think God is in the business of just taking in anyone off the street, do you?"

Eddie turned quickly to head into the very next building, to avoid the woman's glare. As he opened this front door, he noticed that only the pane of glass in the center of it was cracked – everything else appeared to be unscathed, protected almost. Eddie made his way through a foyer that was filled with toolboxes and odd pieces of wood. He pushed through another set of double doors where he found himself in a room that was both dark and empty. He walked down a row of connected oversized seats, folded down the seat on a plush, velvet chair, and sat in it. He closed his eyes and tried to remember the prayers he had learned from the missionaries back in India. He began to talk to God and he felt the presence of someone else. Eddie knew he wasn't alone. That's when a hand grabbed his shoulder. Eddie shrieked. He looked up to see a grim-faced man. The man opened his mouth to reveal two full rows of gold teeth.

"What do you think you're doing in here?"

"I'm here to try to find God."

"Well, I guess it's no harm," the man said as he turned to walk away. "Though, I am in the process of converting the place—it's not a church anymore; it's going to be a bar."

"Oh thank God!" Eddie said and he began to pray in earnest.

···✦✦✦···

To the attention of Crupt:

I was at your very first rally at Nashua State College in 1972 when you ran for your first term. You said then that when you got into office your first order of business would be to do something to fix the "population bomb" before it exploded. You said you didn't want this world to be overrun and its precious resources used up. You said this was more than an environmental issue; you said it was a moral issue that America could no longer choose to ignore. You said you wanted to be part of the solution, not part of the silence.

That was at least 16 terms ago, and I no longer hear you talking about the issue. Now I see from your campaign brochures that you have 6 children.

This is exactly what we get from all of you politicians: a lot of meaningless talk that gets you elected, and a big helping of nothing once you're in office. Nothing ever gets done. Don't you think the citizens of this country deserve a better government in return for their taxes?

Sincerely,
S. Erickson

Dear Mr. or Mrs. Erickson,

Thank you for your letter. It is always good to hear from a constituent, and even better to find out that there are still thoughtful people who take the time to read through campaign brochures and to consider the important issues of the day.

In response to your question, I want to assure you that I am still deeply committed to the causes for which I fought in the 1970s. I am keenly aware that not much has changed in the intervening decades.

Specifically, in regards to overpopulation, I have appointed my 6 children—all of whom have fine minds—to a 6-person committee that studies the problem of population growth and attempts to find solutions. Should the children not come up with an answer to overpopulation in due time, my wife and I stand ready to contribute additional members to this committee—this is how seriously we both take this issue.

Thanks again for taking the time to communicate your concerns.

Sincerely,
P. R. Crupt

Powell R. Crupt took his time to read over the letter one last time, before he added his signature, with a flourish. Then, down at the bottom of the page, he added his motto—which he had distilled (stolen) from Ralph Waldo Emerson: "He who disagrees with himself knows best." Representative Crupt had always made a point of personally responding to all letters received from constituents, ever since he had first been elected to office from Ohio. On this particular day, with Washington D.C. awash in rumors of great tragedy and speculation about the future, he found it most satisfying to retire to his study, unhook the phone, and write back whatever made him happy—to hell with the consequences.

He leaned back in his scarred leather chair (which had been whole before his third youngest, at the age of five, had taken a pair of scissors to it) took a sip of brandy, and listened to the rainfall against the pane of a nearby window. As he sighed, he contentedly reflected on the stack of correspondence to which he had responded.

Just then, the doorbell rang. Crupt sighed again, got to his feet, and stumbled towards the front door. As he opened it, a gust of air pushed in through the opening, and lightning lit up the door's frame. A drenched man, who wore a Brooks Brothers suit, stood on the front stoop.

"Well, Scrodtop, you certainly know how to make an entrance. Why didn't you call?" Crupt asked, without inviting the man to enter his home.

"I've been trying for the past few hours, but I couldn't seem to make a connection," Scrodtop said, as water dripped down his short-cropped dark hair and rolled across his clean-shaven face. "I hope I didn't wake your wife or the children..."

"No, no ... they're back at the cabin in North Dakota—all air travel has been grounded, but, of course, you already knew that. ... I suppose it's for the best, them being in the interior and all."

Scrodtop's face twisted into a frown, as he said, "Yes, well, why don't you invite me in. I'd like to make you president, Mr. Crupt."

"It seems an odd time to be talking about an election, what with you currently serving a sitting president in the midst of a crisis and me wearing a ratty robe and Mickey Mouse slippers," Crupt said as he left the door open and walked back down the hall and on towards the study.

Scrodtop carefully closed the door and followed Crupt, his leather shoes leaving big wet prints everywhere he stepped on the hall's linoleum floor.

"I'm not talking about an election. Haven't you been listening to the news?" Scrodtop replied, as he stepped into the study, crossed the room, and fell into the leather couch underneath the window. "Don't they pay enough in Congress for you to get better furniture? What's with the tape on everything?"

"My son went through an angry stage—he gets that from his mother… What do you mean—you're not talking about an election? I just heard the president say on TV that he had a plan; that no matter how bad things get he would help us see our way through … That he would never cut and run and neither would this nation."

"He just said all that to give his plane time to fuel. As soon as the speech was over, they took the entire Air Force One fleet—with all of the top leaders—and headed out to some underground city in Mongolia. Things are much worse than what he said on TV."

"How could they possibly be worse—he was talking about the end of the world, if we didn't act … ."

"Well, how about the fact that the cloud of ash that was released is going to prevent the sun from rising in the morning, or for at least the next week? How about the string of hurricanes that are about to hit Florida, South Carolina, Louisiana, and

Texas—our scientists say that over 30 million people will die? We have reports of houses being wiped out by hail in the Midwest—entire houses pounded into smithereens by balls of ice that haven't stopped falling. People have no idea which direction to run; we've got freak acts of God killing people left and right all over this globe. Of course, the president did say that this was nothing compared to what will happen with the second set of eruptions, and the stuff he mentioned on TV wasn't close to the stuff he thought would happen here on the East Coast if …"

"Scrodtop, I've been parsing the speech of politicians for over 30 years now in this town. You just said the president 'did say' and 'he thought'—what do you know that you're not telling me? Why didn't you get on that plane with all of the other top aides?"

"Let me just say it this way," Scrodtop whispered, as he leaned towards where Crupt sat in his leather chair, "I have more faith in the work of Dr. Ulent than the president does—I know more about the details of his work. … And maybe I just believe in this country a little more than he does—I believe that somehow America always finds a way, no matter how the odds are stacked against us."

"Scrodtop, I always knew there was something different about you. From the very beginning of this administration, I looked at you—from across the aisle—and said there's a man who doesn't belong with that group," Crupt cut in as he fingered the edge of the armrest on his chair. "Maybe you just aren't as smart as the rest of them. Maybe you should have gotten onto one of those planes."

Scrodtop grimaced as his poker face returned, "You're probably right, Congressman Crupt. But in some places they still call that kind of stupidity patriotism. And I have a feeling you aren't all that much smarter than I am; I saw the manifest—I know you could have been on any one of those planes, had you accepted the invitation. That's why I'm here to offer you the presidency…"

"So now you're the kingmaker. I thought we cleared this up after 9-11. You're insane—last I checked I'm way down on the list of succession …"

"It gets a little fuzzy once you get past Secretary of State. Besides, the top of that list has all gone and so those who are left are the ones that get to move up…"

"And what about the president—you think he's just going to listen to the news of a coup from under Outer Mongolia without responding? And what if your Ulent does what he's supposed to and the world does get saved—what's going to happen when the president comes back?"

"Last I checked it's not a coup if the Commander-in-Chief abandons his post. You were in the military, you know the field rules during combat … Forgive me, Congressman Crupt, but we need to act fast. We have a nation out there without a leader. We have anarchy in the streets. We have already seen over two hundred thousand people die and millions more might be dead before the sun rises again, if it ever does. Those are your people. … Truth is, we're in deep shit, and we need someone who isn't afraid to wade through it.

America needs a hero at this moment, and you're all we've got. Chances are, we're all going to die regardless; but wouldn't you rather go out fighting for something?"

Crupt leaned back and eyed Scrodtop from the top of his wet head to the black-soled bottom of his feet. It was as if he was seeing him for the first time.

"You're right," Crupt said. "I wasn't thinking. It has been as if the whole world out there didn't exist, until this very moment. If this cup has passed to me …"

"I just have two questions to ask."

Crupt leaned forward, suspicious once more. He crossed his arms in front of his chest and smiled a smile that bared his teeth.

"This is beginning to sound like a job interview. What do you got?"

"First, there's Dr. Oppenheimer Ulent. He's working on Plan 51. I know every detail of this plan and I need your commitment that you will let him work, no questions asked. This isn't for his protection; it's for yours."

"This is the same guy who my committee was going to recommend be fired. This is the same guy who got three good scientists killed back up on Mt. St. Helens less than a month ago. This is the same guy who didn't see all of this coming in the first place…"

Crupt stopped, as Scrodtop stood to his feet and began to act as if he was about to walk out of the room, his body leaving a big, wet imprint on the leather surface of the couch.

"Trust me, Ulent knew exactly what was going to go happen; but he couldn't get anyone to listen because Washington D.C. was awash in rumors that he was about to be fired. They all thought he was some crackpot, making stuff up to save his job. He had no power—and even I couldn't get the President to listen under those circumstances." Scrodtop said as he took a step towards a door. "Maybe …"

"Wait," Crupt said as he jumped to his feet and grabbed hold of Scrodtop's arm with both of his hands. "I just wanted to know ... well, I wanted to make sure that nothing ... You know, nothing improper ... well, I guess you're right—the President shouldn't get bogged down with all of the details ..."

"Good!" Scrotop snapped, as he whirled around to face Crupt. "And now, just one more question. How would you deal with all the protestors in the streets? We have reports of riots in every major city. The police have abandoned their posts and mass hysteria has taken hold."

"Well, I should give some sort of press conference. I'll reassure the people that their government is still functioning—that there is a central controlling authority. I'll remind them to be guided by the better angels of their nature and that we all need to pull together ..."

"With all due respect, Mr. Crupt, that doesn't sound like the leader of the free world talking," Scrodtop said, as he took a step out into the hallway. "It's late and I've got a former Supreme Court clerk who is now Chief Justice waiting at the White House to swear in a new American President. I guess I need to double-check that post-9-11 succession plan you mentioned ..."

"No!" Crupt bellowed as he threw his own body in front of that of the departing Scrodtop.

Crupt swallowed hard and began to speak, "Those bastards out there are trying to tear apart the fabric of this nation. They are trying to destroy democracy and our entire way of life. I might just be the only one left who can preserve this great nation of ours. I will immediately issue an executive order declaring martial law. I will order all remaining Army troops—all National Guard units—into the cities to restore order. I will ruthlessly beat back the voice of dissent so that free speech can once again be heard. I will protect and pre-serve democracy, at any cost. I will crack down on anyone who tries to stand in the way of my efforts to restore America to greatness. … Yes, we will be great again … as long as I am President of the United States."

He looked to Scrodtop for some hint of a reaction before continuing, "Out of all of this—out of the ashes—we will emerge, more powerful than ever before. No one will ever dare stand up against me … or this nation, again. America will rise again! I will command the sun to rise!"

"I just had chills run up my spine! Look … there … I've got goosebumps!" Scrodtop exclaimed as he pulled back the arm of his suit jacket. "Please, come with me, sir. We have a lot of work to do tonight … you have a lot of decisions left to make, Mr. President."

···◆◆◆◆◆···

Anna knew that she was extremely fortunate to have gotten a taxi headed into downtown Portland from her apartment. Normally she wouldn't have sprung for such an expensive ride but, between her suicide by sleeplessness and the onset of the end of the world, there didn't seem to be any reason to hold back. Besides she knew that it would have taken the Max much longer to get her to where she was headed. These trains often get stopped by trace amounts of snow and they were doing little better with the thick ash.

Underneath this layer of freshly fallen ash, Portland looked even grayer than usual, like the inside of a fireplace the morn-ing after a rip-roaring fire. The mix of 1930s wood homes, little parks, statues randomly placed on side streets to commemorate people and events with little connection to the area, pizza shops, bakeries, strip clubs, senior center apartments, theaters for live productions, pawn shops, espresso stands, and the rest of it all, Anna saw through the haze as she looked out her passenger window. All of these unrelated buildings intermingled as if the city had been hastily built, year after year, thrown together on a whim, without a hint of zoning or planning or any thought to the future.

There is no future, Anna realized. *This is as far as we get—at least if I can help it. Certainly for me, this is the end. I have reached my last days.*

This thought wasn't frightening or dramatic or significant. It was just one of many thoughts that occurred to her as the ride brought her closer to downtown Portland and her destiny. Death rode with Anna as amiably as any other companion she had ever had in her life, just close enough to seem like they were together but with enough of a distance to keep from experiencing any emotion, to fend off any real connection or attachment.

"Here! This is close enough!" Ana yelled, pushing her door open as the Volvo skidded to a stop. Anna got out, then looked back at the other passengers who had been stuffed there in the back seat of the taxi with her. "I don't understand your language, I don't know your names, I don't know you. Still, I hope you will enjoy a fantastic death." She closed the door, took a step forward, pounded on the front window until it was rolled down, and handed the taxi driver the last of her cash. "I think you say 'Dunkias' to say 'thank you' in your language, so, 'Dunkias!' I doubt you understand a word that I'm saying, but I hope you have the strength to die with dignity. You are off now on your path, as I am on mine. Happy Death to us all!" she added brightly. Then Anna threw on her hood as she turned and walked off in the direction of Pioneer Square.

"Daddy, why did you let that strange woman get into our car with us?" one of the kids in the back seat asked. "I don't know," came the response from the front. "She just hopped in before I could do anything." "So why didn't we stop and flag down a policeman?" asked a woman in the front passenger seat. "She seemed harmless enough," the driver returned. "Why did she act like she couldn't understand what we were saying? And why did she say 'Dunkias' and then hand you a Lizzys Pizza napkin?" "I don't know," the man reiterated. "She was just a strange woman who apparently needed a ride. Sometimes it's good to help strangers in need—especially in times like these.

Now, everybody, let's just pretend like that never happened. ... And lock your doors!" The car started up again, its headlights dimly lighting the street ahead as it rolled out of the story.

·· + ◆ + ··

Ben had been staring at a stain in the green-blue carpet at the Portland airport for the greater part of eight hours, during which time he'd begun to wonder if walking away from an emergency plane landing in the middle of a volcanic eruption was something for which he should be thankful. These musings had been punctuated by bouts of sleep and attempts to stifle his desire to kill every one of the other buffoons in the National Guard unit he was forced to endure.

Ben had devised a method for killing each individual over that time. None were very original—Rieck was to be stabbed repeatedly with the filed metal end of a bootstrap, while First Sergeant Halverson was to be choked by swallowing the cell phone he kept using to try to ascertain the group's orders—but it helped to pass the time.

"There's been a change of plans!" Halverson said as he put his phone in the pocket of his camouflaged pants. The rest of the group, which was in various stages of sprawl around their bags in the abandoned terminal, perked up to hear what Halverson had to say. Cards and portable CD players were set aside. "In light of all that has happened out there today," Halverson continued, "Guess what we get to do?"

"Does it involve those M-16s?" Silver asked.

He pointed at cases of brand new rifles and ammunitions that were being loaded onto armored personnel carriers on the tarmac, just on the other side of the window from where the group sat. Ben looked out the window to see what Silver was talking about. Even with spotlights set up, it was hard to make out what was happening in the black of this particular night.

"That's right, Silver," Halverson said. "They wouldn't give us the new weapons."

"Are those live rounds?" Enrico asked.

"Yup … we get to shoot some people! Guess who?" Halverson could barely contain his excitement.

Just then, Colonel Caifman burst through a side entrance and into the room. Ben and the rest of the soldiers jumped to attention.

"Uncle Sam isn't paying you ladies to play 20 questions!" Caifman barked.

"We weren't, sir. Well, not exactly …" Halverson's voice trailed off.

"That's enough, First Sergeant. It's time to pop some heads in downtown Portland. We're heading to Pioneer Square; there's a big rally going on over there. Where's that chaplain of mine? Major Withers, get out here! Let's pray this group into battle."

A man with white hair who had been trailing Caifman pulled to the front of the group. He knelt and all the soldiers did the same, removing their soft caps as they did so.

Ben felt uncomfortable with the whole thing, so he hung back. He bowed his head but didn't close his eyes. He had joined this unit just after they had come back from their tour of Iraq, but he had heard that these prayer sessions took place before each battle.

"Padgett, get over here! And close your eyes when we talk to the Almighty!" Caifman barked in Ben's direction. Then Caifman turned to the rest of the group, stretched out one of his own long, lean arms, and added, "Get in where you fit in! Put your hands in the God pile!"

All of the soldiers moved together and placed their hands in a pile on top of Caifman's. Ben did the same to avoid any further harassment. It struck him as odd that an Army that is so homophobic had such a wide variety of activities that involved men touching other men.

Major Withers cleared his throat and then his reedy voice sang out, "Dear Lord, we go into battle today against a host of Thine enemies. They bear weapons against Your Holy and chosen nation, they bear seditious signs and chants of hatred for Your Holy American people. We know our cause is just because it is Your cause and the cause selected for us by Your Holy Representative here on earth, the new President of these United States of America…"

Ben's attention was piqued when he heard the words, "new President." He wondered what other news from the outside world he had missed over the past few hours. None of the soldiers had been allowed to contact their relatives in the Portland/Vancouver metro area—Halverson had just muttered something about "morale."

"…and help us to trample out the vintage where the grapes of wrath are born. Help us to tear the enemy from limb to limb with Your great strength. Help us to wisely wield the sword that You sent to earth with Your Holy Son, Jesus Christ. Help us to kick asses and take names, just as He would have done. Let us rock them and sock them and tear out their intestines …"

Colonel Caifman loudly cleared his throat. Withers took a breath and wiped spittle from his cheek with the back of his free hand, his tone becoming more regulated.

"We ask all of this in Your Holy Name, Amen."

"Alright men, load 'em up. Let's get butts to nuts."

The next thing Ben knew, he—and every member of his platoon—had been handed a rifle and together they were sitting in the windowless back of a large armored personnel carrier. He held onto an overhead strap and tried to hear himself think over top of the diesel engine. It seemed like the air was running out, stuck there in the back of the APC with these sweaty men that fingered their rifles and yelled jokes to each other about "popping heads." Instead, Ben wished his head would pop. His head always hurt whenever he was required to ride in the back of an APC, but the pain was all the greater now that he had been forced to don his "brain bucket." Every bump caused his skull to pound against the helmet's Kevlar underbelly.

The APC lurched slowly forward, over top of curbs and debris, in a direction that Ben could only guess at without any windows. He felt the engine's noise descend to a dull roar, and the APC slowly turned into a parked position.

All of the other men stood and piled against the large back opening. Ben could sense the excitement radiating from where they waited back to where he remained huddled in the corner of the metal beast. As the backloading flap fell open, the APC lurched to a complete stop, with the men thrown to the pavement in a clump.

"What are you—a bunch of Keystone Cops?" Colonel Caif called out, as he leaped out of the trail humvee and came up on the scene. "We're here, at the east side of Pioneer Square. Get up and get to your battle positions."

The next thing Ben knew, he was kneeling in the darkness, his shoulder steadied by the rail of a barrier that had been thrown up by the Portland Police, the rifle still in his hands. Behind him by less than 30 yards, stood the Pioneer Courthouse and the street that separated it from the open brick courtyard known as Pioneer Square. Ben—along with all of the Army soldiers from at least 5 different units, Portland Police Officers, and Pioneer Courthouse Security personnel—had their weapons trained on the crowd that was spilling out onto the west side of the square.

Thirty-three hours, Anna thought, as she stood in a crowd at the northwest corner of Pioneer Square. *Goodbye cruel world, you've knocked me around, but I'm going out my way. The end is near and I did it my way.* In the meantime, she had to find ways to keep herself awake. Her quest to find and stop the evil scientists who were trying to save the world had gotten her as far as this corner of Pioneer Square, directly across the street from Nordstrom's and right next to the coffee shop. She found there a sympathetic crowd that had been growing throughout the night. The core of it was the usual Friday protest crowd—a bunch of old hippies and "throw-back" college students who railed against "the war" when one was on and in favor of legalizing marijuana when wars weren't being fought. As of late, many of their protests had been anti- the war on drugs, which had become a perfect issue.

Usually, there were about 50 or so who showed up. They carried signs, had a leader who played the drums to keep them in step, and marched around in a small circle on the Northeastern corner of Pioneer Square—the drug dealers and homeless at the other corners frightened them—until they got too dizzy to carry on.

Tonight, however, they had quickly converted their march into an anti-president, anti-scientist, and anti-saving-the-world unity rally. Their signs had big cross-out marks and hastily written in slogans such as, "Make Love, Not World Salvation," "Live Free and Let the World Die," "No End of the World, No Peace," and "Science, What Is It Good For?"

Since Pioneer Square sits in the heart of downtown Portland, directly across from the Courthouse and the offices for several television stations, the regular group of protestors figured this approach would be the one to guarantee the most media coverage. They were right.

Events flew fast and furious throughout the evening: first the Presidential address had announced pretty much the arrival of the end of the world; then rumors that the President had abandoned the nation were followed by the new president—President Crupt—who had taken to the airwaves to announce that Dr. Ulent was working on a desperate plan (involving nuclear weapons) and finally martial law had been declared. All the while, the crowd had swelled. Now they had several thousand milling around in Portland's "Living Room."

In the thick of it all was Anna. She had found the tallest, blondest, handsomest man in the entire group with whom she now conversed. This being Portland, she figured that there was more than a 50 percent chance that he was gay; but being a newly single young woman on the prowl she was willing to take that those odds.

She had struck up a conversation concerning the weather—which was odd in every way with a steady black dusting of warm ash falling throughout the evening. The man's responses had been pithy, but he hadn't tried to run away. All in all, Anna viewed it as a minor triumph, considering her track record of late. So she moved to a more direct approach and asked the man his name. She figured this was an innocent enough question. The big blonde man just smiled coyly, as he replied quietly, "I'd rather not say."

"Oh—I guess I understand," Anna said, her face turning red as she turned to walk away. Then, taking it personally, she thought better of it and decided to give this gorgeous hulk a piece of her mind. Turning back to face him, she launched into a tirade, "I might not be your type—because I'm the wrong hair color, too short, the wrong gender, or whatever ... But you've got no right to just refuse to respond in a civilized way … What I mean is you don't know that I'm asking because I just broke up with my boyfriend and I'm trying to get back at him by finding the first available man so I can … Well, I can't even believe you would think I'm some sort of cheap hussy…"

All the while, the blonde stranger kept waiting for an opening to interject something, but Anna just kept rolling over the top of his "excuse me's" with her breathless monologue. Finally, he took more extreme measures. He reached out and placed the length of his long index finger across her thin lips.

Anna wanted to be angry and wanted to keep talking. But, she also found that she liked having the warm skin of his finger touch her face. So she listened as he said, "You misunderstand. It's not that I don't want to tell you my name—it's just that my name is embarrassing. It always has been for strangers."

"Oh," Anna said as he removed his finger from her mouth brushing it against her cheek in the process, "Then I guess I take back most of what I just said and I'll sneak off now."

"Yes, you should take back most of what you said, but don't leave; and who the hell still uses the word 'hussy' anymore, anyway?" He smiled, but not in the sort of way that indicated he was having fun at her expense. In fact, with his white teeth set against the black haze, he looked like the very image of innocence.

"So, what is your name? It can't be all that embarrassing…"

"Let me just put it this way—it was enough to get me both pantsed and shoved into my PE locker when I changed junior high schools one winter term. By the time a janitor finally freed me, three hours later, every part of me had turned blue—and I mean every part of me. That's the kind of treatment only reserved for the worst freaks—that's exactly what you're looking at: a Grade-A Freak."

"It can't be all that bad," Anna persisted, convinced that there was nothing freakish about this gentle giant.

"Well, don't say I didn't warn you," he said, as he extended his long muscular arm to shake her hand. "The name is Dick. … My honest to God birth-certificate name. See, people always promise, and then they end up doing exactly what you're doing—trying to hold back a giant grin…"

"No, no … it's a strong name, a good name. Oh, come on—it's no worse than my name, Anna—I got made fun of plenty. They've called me 'Anna Vagina,' 'Anal Anna' … and the like—see, now you're laughing at me."

"No, I just had a strange thought—if someone was listening in on us they might make some sort of funny joke about the fact that Dick is hanging out with 'Anal Anna.'"

Anna grinned back, "OK, so how did you get the name? Is it *really* Richard or Rick and your parents just had a sadistic streak—something like a 'Boy Named Sue'…"

Dick's eyes lit up with surprise, "A woman who knows her Johnny Cash and who manages to insert him appropriately into a conversation. The world must be ending for there to be such a beautiful thing…"

"It's just that my boyfriend …" Anna stopped herself, conscious of a look that flashed across her new companion's face, before carefully continuing, "My *ex*-boyfriend listened to him every time he wanted to… Well, it's a long story and it involves all sorts of cross-dressing, so I think I'll stop now before I say something socially unacceptable. … You were about to explain the name …"

Dick smiled, appreciative of the lengths to which Anna had just gone to make it clear that she was available. He edged closer to her, the belt on his black overcoat brushing up against her hand.

"Yes, I would have been better off with Rick or Richard, but the name on my birth certificate *really* is just Dick. My mom is from Norway so she didn't understand … Anyway, she was reading 'Do Androids Dream of Electric Sheep' when she bumped into my dad on the New York subway. … That's the one that was made into 'Blade…'"

"…Runner." Anna blurted out before Dick could finish.

A frown furled Dick's lean face as he asked, "Your boy-friend again?"

His face snapped back into place as Anna reassured him, "No…that's all me. I love stuff from the old days—the 1980s and 90s. … Say, did you hear what is being said?" She gestured towards the bottom step at the amphitheater end of Pioneer Square—close to the southwest corner. She tugged at the unbuttoned flap of Dick's overcoat and started in that direction. He followed her and the pair crossed directly through the middle of the square, walking between the speaker and the police barricades set off in the distance.

"…We might be a nonviolent movement, but we can't just let them roll over us. It's time to take back the courthouse from those fascists who have moved in!" a dark-skinned woman dressed in a sari screamed through a megaphone at the crowd as she gestured at the police barricades.

No one seemed to know exactly why Pioneer Courthouse needed to be taken; but, with the end of the world approaching, this particular crowd didn't need much convincing. Led by this woman—whose last protest leadership position had been with the Weathermen Underground some 40 years before—the crowd obediently turned to face the barricades, with no idea as to what lay on the other side.

"Hey, hey … ho, ho! This fucked up world has got to go!" someone began to chant and the rest of the crowd took it up as they slowly advanced, three-thousand strong.

Anna shivered. She didn't know if it was because she was tired or because she was suddenly scared. Unwittingly, because of the route she had taken to get to the center of Pioneer Square, she now found herself at the head of an angry mob about to confront the police … or worse.

Dick saw her tremble. He stretched out his hand and took hers in his. She liked the warmth of it and its weight. Anna looked up at him and smiled. "I'm in the process of committing suicide by sleep deprivation!" she yelled to him, trying to be heard over top of the crowd. Either he didn't hear or didn't understand, because Dick smiled back and mouthed the words, "good luck." Then he took up the crowd's chant, which had changed. It was now "Live free or die!" They yelled the chant of independence in unison, as if it rose from one giant throat.

From behind the police barricade line, Ben shivered—despite the warmth of the night. He leaned against the wooden barrier and wondered how he had gotten himself into this mess. He had the safety locked on his rifle, even as Colonel Caif paced behind the group and ordered, "Scan your lane and aim! Don't fire until I give the …" Directly beside him lay Private Rieck, a pumpkin-faced grin spread across the width of his face. As Caif had said the word "fire," he squeezed off a shot, the crackle from that single round of rifle fire demanding to be heard despite the chant of the crowd. As it reverberated, the night grew still.

Someone in the front lines of the crowd—now no more than 20 yards from where Ben leaned—shrieked. With a sick feeling in the pit of his stomach, Ben watched the reaction. People screamed and fell to the ground.

People lay in piles all around Anna. She felt herself being yanked downward by Dick's weight. She curled closer to him on the brick-covered ground of the square. She noticed that he was sweating, profusely. *Do all men sweat like pigs?* Anna wondered as she drew the sleeve of her sweat jacket back and found that it was sopping wet. The liquid had a strange color and consistency. She looked more closely at Dick, who hadn't moved. The left side of his scalp had been shot clean off. All that remained was a burned and bleeding hole above his left eye socket. Anna stared at her new companion who was no more. A light dusting of ash was beginning to cover his pale skin.

All around her people whimpered. They lay there on the ground.

Anna, however, found that all fear had left her body. She took to her feet. Inside of her Anna felt anger boiling – anger directed at a world that wouldn't die no matter how much it deserved its fate, directed at lovers who hinted at commitment but abandoned her, directed at a society that humiliated a man because they thought his name was strange, directed at cowards who shot into crowds from behind barriers, directed at injustice, directed at hate-filled fascist police, directed at power-hungry politicians, directed at life, directed at God, at the mountains and the very earth upon which she stood.

Anna turned to face the barricade. She raised her fist and unfurled her middle finger. As if on cue, the crowd around began to rise. There was no longer any need for speeches, nonviolent chants, or causes to justify their actions. All at once, they found the only motivation that was ever really needed to forge a collective movement. Following Anna's example, the mob was roused by rage, vengeance, and hate.

They charged towards the barricades. Back behind the lines, Caif awakened, as if from a trance. "Fire! Fire! Kill them, you fools!" Ben heard him call out. It was too late. The mob had already arrived at the table and was ready to eat. Without thinking, Ben jumped to his feet. All along the line, his comrades did the same. With no way to get off a safe shot without killing their own, it was hand-to-hand combat, of the fiercest kind. Faces met fists, and knee caps met feet. Arms, legs, heads, chests, thighs, teeth, backs, ears, skull bones, elbows, and fingernails all flew into the fray. Asses clumped up against assholes in a melee where one body blended into the next. There was no male, no female, no black, no white, no gay, no straight—just angry bodies locked in a life and death struggle in the dark of night.

Ben, who had been trying valiantly to defend himself, found his position overrun. His helmet ripped from his head, he was being pummeled—arms and legs freely flying at him from all directions. He was pushed to the ground, the forward push of the unthinking thick of the crowd trampling the leading edge. Soon Ben was lying on the ground, a pile of bodies crushing down on him.

Then Ben felt something move between his thighs. He looked down between his legs and saw the pixie-face of a woman there. Her eyes locked onto his. She burrowed her head against the bulge between his legs. He could feel her face and then her lips. Ben felt a sharp pain as the woman sank her teeth through his camouflaged pants and into his skin. He screamed as the world around him went black.

Anna's head snapped up and she snarled, "This is for you, Dick!" the crowd piling over her. As she felt the weight of human bodies falling upon her, Anna desperately struggled to keep from losing consciousness.

III - There is Nothing New Under the Sun

*O*ut there, the earth is just another piece of cosmic garbage, floating on the edge of a cesspool. It is a piece of shit, discharged from a celestial asshole billions of years ago. All intelligent beings now understand that human lifeforms cling to a piece of space debris on the edge of one galaxy among many. There is nothing special about our particular rock. Yet, we persist in believing that there is something special about us. First, we boldly proclaimed that we were created in God's image. Now that this has been proven false (a fact that millions of Americans, but no large numbers in any other Western nation, still inexplicably deny), we try to insist that we are of a higher order—that we are the cream of the crop produced by natural selection.

I've seen it in charts on classroom walls, which depict bacteria becoming fish becoming birds becoming apes becoming Homo sapiens. Hunters and gatherers turned to farming; agriculture led to communities; cities led to the rise of great nations; behold Western Civilization and our way of life.

I write today to tell you that it just isn't so. Humans are not the end result of predictable evolutionary progress but rather a cosmic afterthought, a tiny little twig on the bush of life, which, if replanted from seed, would *almost surely not grow this twig again, or perhaps any twig with any property that we could care to call consciousness. Evolution is not inherently progressive; it does not work toward "higher" good; it does not act "for" the benefit of groups as species or communities; it does not produce desired ends: harmonious ecosystems and well-designed organisms. We are not progressing in a sensible direction, nor are we the result of such progress. Any belief you hold to the contrary is wrong.*

Natural selection acts only for the benefit of individuals in reproductive success. Strip away society with all its rules—peel away jobs, book learning, bank accounts, and marriages—and all that is left is a desire, a need, to survive in order to fuck.

Well-designed organisms and balanced ecosystems emerge as side consequences. Order is only a side consequence of the "invisible hand" of evolution; all direct causality resides in the struggle among individuals for survival.

As I write these words, my desk is covered in stacks of reports sent to me by scientists around the world. These papers detail the current state of the world. At this very moment, a tsunami is striking the Eastern Coast of America; with that, the waters of the Atlantic will rise up and swallow stretches of civilization between New York and Atlanta. In other places, balls of ice are smashing cities to smithereens in the Midwest. Above us, a hole in the ozone layer has been ripped wide open. The polar ice caps are melting at a rate that will soon lead to the permanent submersion of coastlands on every continent; no coastal region will be spared the effects, from the Pacific Islands to India, from the Ivory Coast to Greenland.

This will all worsen with the simultaneous eruptions in the Cascade Range that will produce ash clouds that will hang over it all. These clouds will obscure the light from the sun around the globe. The next wave of eruptions will sever the Pacific Coast—Baja California to the Great Northwest—from North America. There the sea will swallow the shore whole. Catastrophe will follow. The earth will be plunged into permanent darkness. Our rock will burn from the heat and then grow cold once more.

I am the only one who can find a way for humanity to claw out of this shit. I hold the knowledge that this world needs to survive. This is as it has always been. Science has given us light to turn night into day. Science held off the dark shadows of both fascism and communism with one spectacular blow in Hiroshima. Science has given us bodies that live to old age without the loss of mental or sexual vigor. Science has allowed us to fly, to run without growing weary, and to communicate across the distance. Science has created a prosperous global way of life. Science has even provided for us a way off this rock.

Now, science, using me as the instrument, will prevent us all from sliding back into primordial ooze. Once again, it comes back to one individual who might just, as a consequence of his work, save the entire species. Scientific knowledge is not a greater or higher good; in this cesspool, it is the only good.

Oppenheimer Ulent was startled out of his contemplations by the ring of the phone. He put down his pen, closed up his leather-bound notebook, and took the receiver in his hand.

"Yes… Hello, Scrodtop. I've been expecting your call. Of course, I heard the announcement.

…Fine, fine, I'll admit it. You were right… Yes, hook, line, and sinker. I would have loved to have seen his face when you told him… Well, of course, do be sure to thank our new President for his confidence in me.

…It's all set …yes, tomorrow. No, nothing will go wrong.

…Yes, I heard that. Just tell them cabin fever or something for now. After tomorrow, I'll give them a proper scientific explanation.

…OK, so, yes, that's two things! Yes, the labs at UW keep pointing that out to me…of course, I had the data already set up with Puget Sound figured in; one of my assistants just sent it out when the chain …

…Fine, fine, but I haven't received it. What number did you send it to? … No, that's my old fax number, from OPU—I haven't used that in years. … Well, the one here should be on the bottom of page two of the Eiler draft…yes, that's it— I'm sure. I'll get hold of someone there and make sure that it doesn't wind up in the wrong ….

…OK, I'll let you handle that end of it. Right now, I have the world to save."

···◆◆◆···

Anna gripped hold of the leg on the body beneath her. It was being pulled out from below the stack of people. She closed her eyes as she was wedged out of the human pile. Once she felt the body stop moving, she opened her eyes and looked up. She saw that she had been dragged to the sidewalk in front of the Pioneer Courthouse by a soldier with a name tag that read "Rieck." She let go of the leg she had been holding, which Anna now realized belonged to another soldier. Rieck had been trying to revive his fallen comrade. Anna saw Rieck's lips move towards the other soldier's mouth. He was using a mouth-to-mouth resuscitation technique.

Anna rolled to her feet and ran back towards Pioneer Square. Behind her, she heard a man's voice yelling, "Retreat!" In front of her, she saw the woman with the megaphone trying to restore order to the mob. "We've won!" the woman yelled.

"The fascists are gone. Stop shoving! People are going to die if you don't stop shoving!"

After several minutes of chaos, the crowd finally began to listen. A great cheer greeted the realization that the soldiers and police had retreated. "Alright, let's get a team together to gather up all of the weapons that we've taken," the sari-clad woman ordered; then she added, "We're going to beat them into plowshares!" The crowd roared in delight. At least half of them thought a "plowshare" was some fascist police officer they would soon have the chance to beat. The woman fed off of the excitement of the crowd as she continued, "Let's get another team to carry out the wounded ..." She paused, looked towards the center of Pioneer Square, and added, "...and the dead."

The crowd went silent, as people strained to see the body of their martyr. Anna couldn't bear to look in that direction. The silence was broken, as the woman threw in, "But mark my words: this sacrifice was not made in vain. He gave his life so that this world might die, and we'll carry on the fight!" The crowd screamed in delight once more. Anna noticed that the woman spoke with an accent; she held out her vowels longer than most English speakers and clipped her ending consonants. It made for an oddly hypnotic mix.

"All of our lives, all of our civilization, humankind has bent the earth to its wishes. We've obliterated its natural resources, we've enslaved our fellow animals, and we've genetically altered the plant life. These sins are upon the heads of us all!" The crowd cheered, although somewhat less enthusiastically. It seemed that responsibility was a tough cross to bear.

"And now, the earth has spoken back! Hear its voice in the mountains, in the spread of lava and ash that threaten to erase our existence—our entire civilization—from the face of the earth! The earth speaks in hailstorms in the Midwest, hurricanes on the East Coast, and flooding throughout Europe! Now, when the earth is trying to speak, are we going to let the fascist pigs silence her voice?" The crowd burst into sustained applause throughout her monologue. Now, they roared back an enthusiastic "Hell No!"

"Are we going to let the scientists—who gave us the atom bomb, who gave us chemical and biological weapons, who gave us genetically altered tomatoes, and who gave us Nazi extermination camps and genocide throughout the world, including in the country of my birth... Are we going to let those scientists silence the voice of the earth?"

As the energy of the crowd swelled within her, Anna found herself cheering as loudly as the rest. Her voice blended in with thousands of others, screaming "Hell No!"

"Join with me in helping the earth rise against her masters! Join with me in putting a stop to Dr. Oppenheimer Ulent who wants to shove nuclear bombs up the earth's vagina! Join with me in letting the voice of the earth be heard loud and clear, now and forever!" The crowd went wild. Beneath the black haze, with the wounded and dead strewn about them, people were jumping up and down, screaming wildly, and giving each other high-fives.

"Follow me up the street to OPU and Anarchy Hall!" the woman finished. She made large gestures toward the hill to the south of where they all currently stood. Slowly the crowd began to break up and head in the direction that the woman had indicated. Anna stayed behind waiting to be sure that someone picked up the body of Dick before she turned to follow the crowd. By this point, Pioneer Square was left as empty as Anna herself. *It's not like I knew the guy…* she thought, as she crossed the street in front of First Patriotism Bank.

In the middle of the street, she was nearly mowed over by a speeding Mercedes SUV as it zipped forward in the dark. Anna jumped to get out of the way and screamed an obscenity at the vehicle. She raised her finger to flip off the driver. As she did so, a twinge of sadness shot through her. The reverse lights on the SUV—which bore rear bumper stickers that read "I brake for bugs" and "Don't you dare open the Antarctic to drilling!"—flashed on, lighting up the black haze. Anna realized that it was backing up. This wasn't quite what she had intended. She might have been in the middle of committing suicide, but she still wasn't particularly interested in being pummeled to death by an irate motorist. She ducked back onto the sidewalk, just as the SUV crossed back in front of her. The passenger-side window rolled down. "Hey, I don't want any trouble," Anna said, as she lifted her arms and held her palms out flat. "All I want to do is …"

"You're the one who with that big blonde guy…the man who was shot," the dark-skinned woman on the passenger side of the car called out, "You're the one who led the charge! I didn't recognize you until I looked in the rearview mirror and saw you flip us off…. Do you need a ride?"

Anna recognized the sari-clad woman who had wielded the megaphone. She started towards the rear door. "Sure," she said, taking hold of the handle. "I could use a ride. I've been up for about 35 hours now, and I know it's quite a walk." As Anna slid onto the leather seat, the woman turned to face her from the passenger seat. She smiled. "I'm Bindi," she said, and then pointed to the driver—another woman with short cut blonde hair and large purple triangle earrings. "This is Astral. She is my ... she's my roommate." Astral, who smiled at Anna as the introduction got underway, now frowned and glared at Bindi. Without a word, she gunned the engine. The SUV lurched forward. Bindi turned down the radio, as she strained to hear Anna over top of the newscast.

"I'm Anna. Are the two of you students at OPU?"

"Oh, no," Bindi replied with a laugh. "I'm the Dean of Student Services and Astral is head of Germanic Lit. Are you a student?"

"Well, I used to be. Now I go to ... another college..."

"Oh... which one?"

"Um... Herald Junior College—it's a good school."

"Herald ... I don't think I've heard of that one," Bindi said, as she turned to Astral. "Have you heard of it?"

"No, *roomie*, I haven't," Astral said sharply as she switched off the radio and looked at Anna through the mirror in the center of the windshield to continue. "So, Anna, have you heard the latest?"

"No—I was just waiting there at Pioneer Square for ... well, I was just waiting. I haven't had a chance to hear anything."

"Well, there's something weird happening with survivors from out near the mountains. They're marching onto the cities, which the police and army have mostly abandoned; the radio even said something about reports of a large group from Mt. Hood headed here," Bindi said.

Astral added, "They've had protests all across the nation, in every major city and on just about every campus! Over

40,000 people showed up at Evergreen to symbolically pour red Jell-O into the Puget Sound. They burned down the Army Recruitment office at Harvard and stoned the Dean of Medicine at Yale—it's revolution time, Baby!"

"Yes, yes, it's what we've been waiting for," Bindi broke in. "But I hope that we can maintain the non-violent character of our movement—even if we have to bend the rules a little."

"Sure," Astral said sourly. "We don't want to break too many societal conventions at a time like this. We want to maintain nice, moral lives as the world ends. We shouldn't say, or do, anything that might cause gossip, now should we … roomie?"

"So, just what is the plan?" Anna asked, trying to quickly change the subject. "Are we going to march into Dr. Ulent's house and lynch him?"

"His house … Oh, no, I don't think so," Bindi said, looking back at Anna. "We might compose a letter to express our dissatisfaction and tape it to the front of his lab at OPU…"

"He has a lab there?" Anna asked. "I thought he was head of some big agency in Washington D.C.?"

"Yes, but he had a lab named in his honor after he left the faculty here. I wouldn't want to…"

Astral cut in, "What my roommate is trying to say is that Ulent is still a big shot on our campus. He was in town just a month ago for that Mt. St. Helens thing, wining and dining. We wouldn't want to offend the wrong people as we take over the world, now would we?"

"It would be a *strongly* worded letter…" Bindi objected, as Astral steered the SUV onto the front lawn of the OPU Graduate Library and cut through a bed of flowers. "Slow up please! Would you try not to kill all of our seeded fellow beings … Well, anyway, here we are."

Astral pulled the SUV to a stop, knocking over a sign that read "Dr. Weiler's Peace and Memorial Garden". "Wow!" exclaimed Anna, as she bounded out of the back seat of the car. "That giant woodchuck statue must have been put up since I was thr … since I left this college. It's so beautiful!" As the other women got out of the SUV they looked up into the empty space between buildings where Anna was staring. "Woodchuck statue?" Bindi whispered to Astral. "I told you that you were driving too fast. You've jostled our young comrade's brain."

···◆◆◆◆◆···

Jon Glitzka drove into downtown Portland from across Broadway Bridge with one hand on the steering wheel while he reached his other arm out of the cab of his truck. In his hand was a rag he used to wipe the winshield. Black streaks smudged the glass. Ash layered the ebony skin on his arm. The cracked fingernails on his hands were almost as black as the smudge-covered rag.

Jon steered wide around the corner at the west end of the bridge. He pulled his big rig in front of a building with a neon sign that read, "McNorman's and Smith's Eatery." This early Saturday morning, just before one am, the parking spaces along the street were almost empty. There was an old Ford truck up the street that was covered in ash. A red BMW nearby looked to have just pulled into a space in front of the restaurant since it was only lightly dusted. There was no hint of moonlight. The solid layer of grime on the ground was capped by thick clouds in the sky. A streetlight flickered on and off overhead at the front of the truck. A hefty man in a white chef's jacket leaned out of the eatery's front door and smiled, "So you finally made it. I had almost given up on you—what took you so long?" Jon, with a chuckle, called back, "What the hell do you think?" The man in the doorway leaned back into the restaurant and yelled, "I'm gonna need a couple of you to help Jon unload out here. Sampson … and Sarducci, get out here, now!"

The white-jacketed man then walked out towards the cab of the truck with his hand extended. Jon shook it. Behind him, two men in pink jackets and matching ball caps ran towards the back of the truck's trailer.

"Well, Jimmy, that was some trip, let me tell you. I went out to that ranch in John Day, just like we planned, and picked up all that meat. Then I says to myself, 'I think I'll go through the mountains, instead of I-84, to avoid all those weigh stations.' What with the irregularities in the paperwork and all…"

"Oh, so you got it…"

"Yeah, I got it alright, and it looks like some premium cuts. Anyway, normally I would have taken the Washington side, but something deep inside me told me not to—of course, now I know that I'd be deep under that lava had I gone that way."

"You'd at least be still on the road driving—they're detouring everyone on that side around Seattle."

"Yes sir. Anyhow, so I'm just below the Mt. Hood Ski Resort when the eruption hits. I was sitting there at this coffee shop when all of a sudden I hear … well, I don't know. The closest I can say is that it sounded like when Uncle Sam sent me out to this island in the Pacific and we all watched the French drop an atom bomb over the Bikini Atoll."

Jon stopped to shake his head. He spat onto the curb of the street, expelling thick black juice.

"Isn't that something—how God's fireworks match those set off by men? There was the same kind of flash of light and then this sticky heat—everything just kind of shook up. The next thing I know, we got boulders and snowdrifts all around us blocking the road.

"That must have been something to see..."

"Yeah, and to feel and hear and taste," Jon said as he paused to spit again. "Well, I spent about four hours going out with the owner of the restaurant to check on some of the locals—all the while, they got life flight helicopters coming in to get the wounded and the dead. It took another two hours to dig out my rig. After that, I was back on the road and headed here."

Behind them, there was the sound of a chain clanking against a metal surface. The back of the trailer had been opened.

"It looks like you ran out of windshield cleaning fluid."

"Sure did. Yeah, I ran out of it about halfway down. It was just the craziest mix of sleet and ash—even darker up there than down here, with all sorts of things to steer around in that road. I still can't believe I made it out." Jon said as he paused to wipe his eyes clean.

"I don't even know why I'm keeping the restaurant open in this hell. I guess we're all just working to keep our minds off of it."

"Yeah, that's what it is—just keeping your mind busy, you know…"

A voice called out from the back of the truck, "Hey, Jimmy, you'd better come to take a look back here!"

"Just a second," Jimmy said, as he turned away from Jon and went running towards the back of the truck.

A few moments later, Jimmy yelled, "What the hell?"

Jon slowly turned and walked back to see what the commotion was. As he turned the corner at the end of the truck's trailer, he saw Jimmy with his finger pointing into the back of the truck. The two men in pink hats were just staring.

"This isn't meat!" Jimmy exclaimed. "At least not the kind I'm going to serve to my customers!"

"What are you talking 'bout? I had a full load of meat when I left John Day," Jon began as he tried to peer through the trailer's opening and into the dark shadows. As his eyes adjusted, Jon gasped. He took a step forward to make sure he was seeing what he thought he saw. Inside of the refrigerated back of the truck sat what appeared to be men, women, and children; they were arranged in row after row. They looked pale and gaunt. They looked to be alive. Several were shivering. All of them had their eyes closed.

"Well, I'll be—it's like what I saw in that village … the one that was too close …"

Jimmy cut off Jon with a hiss, "Look at their skin … and all around them…"

Jon leaned in to take a closer look. There was blood smeared on their bodies—on their faces, arms, and bellies. There was blood dripping from the walls and ceiling of the trailer. Jon slowly reached out his hand to touch the face of a woman who sat on the very edge of the trailer's opening. His trembling black fingers moved towards her white face. It was a face as pure as that of the Virgin Mary. His fingers made contact. "Oh dear God..." Jimmy whispered, as he slowly took another step back and away from the truck. "Their eyes are opening—look at their eyes..." From front to back, all of those humans—all at the same time—opened their eyes. Jon stood there, his arm still extended, paralyzed by fear. He stared towards the back of the trailer, mesmerized by those eyes. Then he felt a sharp pain in his fingers. He looked back towards his outstretched hand, the one he had placed on the woman's face. Two of his fingers were now missing. He screamed. "Run!" Jimmy screeched. "Run!"

··✦✦✦✦··

Anna turned all the way around as she oriented herself to the surroundings. She looked down the hillside at the lights from the city's high-rise buildings. Portland's skyline looked very different now, swathed in a black haze and with fewer lights than normal. Anna hadn't set foot on the campus since she'd been thrown out by Sparnell; back then, she had walked across the college and enjoyed the nighttime view. That was one of her best memories of OPU.

Old Peeuuw—as it was affectionately called by the first classes of graduating students—had been founded in the 1950s at the height of the move from GI to civilian life after World War II. Back then, Oregon's Portland University had been lauded as the West Coast's answer to the Ivy League. All of the buildings had been built to enhance the view of the Central

Cathedral, a large stone structure with stained glass windows (featuring the saints of education—Freud, Dewey, Nietzsche, Hegel, Marx, Rousseau, Descartes, Locke, Machiavelli, Aristotle, Socrates, Plato, Confucius, and Eisenhower), gargoyles on every parapet (formed to resemble the devils of education—Hitler, Stalin, Mao, Alexander the Great, Henry the VIII, Genghis Khan, Castro, and nearly every other leader who had ever tried to put into practice a vision espoused by one of the saints of education), with ivy covering just about every square inch of it.

The three women stood in front of a wood and glass building that had been constructed in the early 1970s. In 1969, the hippies had taken to the campus and demanded that the OPU College President yield to their ideas of how best to run the world. In response, the OPU College Administration had offered them "Anarchy Hall" (the anarchist movement always had a large following in Oregon, likely because the state also has one of the highest unemployment rates in the nation).

Now, forty years later, they were going to collect on the original demand made of the college—total control of the world. At least five hundred people had managed to stagger up the hill in the dark to find the place.

"I told you to have an extra set of keys made up," Astral muttered, as Bindi unlocked the doors to the hall to let them all in.

Once inside, Anna (who had never before been in the place, since she had never seen any of the other regular students go into the building—just burnt-out yuppies) discovered a brightly painted interior that shone brightly under the fluorescent, overhead lights. The interior walls were covered with murals of an imagined future for humanity: inner-city gang members handed out condoms and clean needles to farm kids in overalls, Yippies cheerfully pumped ethanol gas for flower children in Beemers, priests and nuns passed out population control literature to Canadian Mounties, while Republicans danced naked around a maypole (you could identify them by the rainbow-colored "I Like Ike" tattoos on their fat asses).

The crowd filed in and sat on the cold, wooden pews (which had been donated by the Unitarian Church in downtown Portland during their remodel in 1987). Bindi descended into the well of the auditorium to speak. Anna found that—despite what she might have guessed—the anarchists (who formed the core group of protestors) were quite adept at running meetings. They had a system worked out that allowed everyone to be heard, sometimes 2 or 3 times, before any decision could be made. They had a sophisticated voting scheme that prevented anyone from voting in blocs, or trading votes. This decision-making apparatus had evolved to the point where not one single decision had been made since 1993 (when it had finally been agreed that the group should support Jimmy Carter in his presidential bid).

This was to be Anna's greatest challenge in her bid to commit suicide by sleep deprivation: hour after hour of speeches concerning the "next step." The anarchists also spent a great deal of time arguing about arcane points of their unique parliamentary procedure. Anna quickly learned that many of the other folks were faculty members and administration at OPU. She wondered how these people ever managed to make decisions back at the faculty senate or on curriculum committees.

She kept taking trips to the restroom to splash her face with water to keep awake. This was the best part of the whole proceeding as the anarchists in line for the bathroom in the hallways reveled in telling jokes. There were many that Anna overheard, including the following:

> Sentient Being 1: How many anarchists does it take to screw in a light bulb?
> Sentient Being 2: I don't know, how many?
> Sentient Being 1: None. Anarchists don't do any screwing.

> and

> Sentient Being 1: Say, have you heard the one about the anarchist who got laid?
> Sentient Being 2: No, I haven't heard about the anarchist who got laid …
> Sentient Being 1: Well, of course, you haven't … it never happened!

In between trips to the restroom, Anna found that most of the discussion revolved around whether or not the group should head to the zoo and set loose all of the animals. Anna still wasn't sure of the reasons for this endeavor, even as the crowd finally proceeded to vote. The best argument, in favor of the motion, seemed to be the fact that the zoo was "right next door." Suddenly, just when it looked like the measure was certain to pass, a young man came running into the room. At first, Anna could swear that she saw a woodpecker tapping at his head. She rubbed her eyes, looked again, and realized that it was just a large, flapping cowlick.

"PETA set all of the zoo animals free," he yelled. This news caused quite a stir. Accusing whispers reverberated around the room. "They beat us again!" one of the anarchists screeched angrily. "That's so unfair! It just seems like every other group is better organized than we are!"

Anna had finally had enough. She had now been up for over 40 hours, according to a large clock on the wall (the anarchists wanted to keep track of just how anachronistic they were). Not one who would normally speak up, Anna marched to the front of the room and stepped directly in front of Bindi. With her death imminent one way or the other, Anna was fully ready to throw caution to the wind. "Look at the time!" she said, gesturing at the clock. Then she walked across the stage and to a window at the side of the room. As dramatically as she could, she pulled down on the blind and let it sharply spring upward and open. "Look," she yelled. "It's daylight!"

Gasps filled the room. Anna's dramatic gesture was ruined by the fact that it was still dark outside. Through the pane of glass, Anna thought she could see an elephant that was trumpeting as it passed. She did a double-take, and it was gone. "Is that clock wrong?" a man asked before the woman beside him leaned over to remind him of the situation. "What I mean is, the world is about to end and we're just sitting here!" Anna said, struggling to regain her composure. "Are we just going to let the scientists save this world without trying to stop them?"

"Hell no!" Astral's voice rang out before she realized that she was the only one who replied.

"Now, look people. I know Dr. Ulent's home address. He lives right down the road in Lake Oswego and we can march to his house and … and…" As Anna struggled to finish her sentence—to tell this crowd exactly what they would do once they reached Ulent's house—Bindi broke in. She turned to the crowd. "This is exactly the sort of information we've needed so that we can take meaningful action." she declared. Astral leaped to her feet, her fists in the air. "All those in favor of Anna going to Dr. Ulent's house—to stop him from saving the world—raise your hands!" The motion carried. The group cheered and the meeting broke up.

As people took to their feet to leave the room, a tall bearded man approached Anna. He had a crumpled piece of paper in his outstretched hand. "I don't know if it will help, but I think you might want to take a look at this," he whispered, as he handed the paper to Anna. "I work in Ulent's old office—this was sent to his old fax number by mistake. I was ordered to shred it."

Distracted Anna looked at the paper. It just looked like a series of numbers. She folded it and put it in the pocket of her sweat jacket. "Don't lose it," the bearded man hissed. "It shows exact times and locations for the nuclear blasts planned by Dr. Ulent. Trust me; you'll want to read it … carefully…" Then the man slipped out a side door.

Just like that, Anna was left alone on stage. She pulled out her cell phone, "I meant we could do something together, as a group…" she muttered in the direction of the retreating crowd. She then selected a number from her electronic contact list and hit the "send" button. She lifted the phone to her ear and listened to it ring.

"Hello … yes, it's me. No, I haven't died yet. …I need to see you. No, not…well, I'll explain when I see you. Just bring everything you can find on Dr. Ulent—especially that '51 Ways' list. …Yes, fine. …I'll meet you at Pioneer Place Mall, then. …Well, I don't know. Just meet me at the Game Wild Store! …Just be there! I've got something important to do, and I might just be the only one in the world who can get it done." She clicked the "end" button on her phone, and put it back in the pocket of her hooded sweat jacket; right next to the piece of paper the bearded man had handed her. With just about everyone gone, Anna felt almost entirely alone.

"Well, at least I still have you here to help me," Anna said, turning towards a giant spotted walrus that lay on the floor beside her. The walrus grunted twice then kazooed. "Okay, okay, I wouldn't want you to miss your aunt's step mom's birthday!" Anna yelled after her, as the walrus faded into the concrete. "Just leave me here all by myself! See if I care! … You wouldn't have been much help without opposable thumbs in any case!"

Now Anna really was entirely alone. She felt the full weight of the end of the world on her shoulders.

··•♦•♦•··

"Are you lonesome, today?" Eddie asked the red-haired receptionist. He had a broad smile on his freshly scrubbed face. "What with it being Saturday and the end of the world and all, you must be the only person in the world who has to work." Eddie was on a mission. He had hitchhiked miles to get from Camas to his family's home in Portland, which required a harrowing journey across the Columbia River by way of the Bridge of the Gods, before continuing his trek here. Still, he had time to flirt. "Actually, here at Ulent Labs OPU we've been working around the clock. Now, what was the name you were looking for?" the receptionist matter-of-factly responded to Eddie's friendly banter.

"It's my brother, Ulysses Chandran. My dad wanted me to check in on him … we've lost touch, but last we knew he worked here," as he spoke Eddie's fingernails drummed on the marble countertop that formed the receptionist's shield from the public. She had a microphone/earphone stuck to the side of her face, tucked underneath her long red mane. She turned to face her computer monitor. Her fingers moved quickly across the keyboard.

"That's 'Shandran' … with an 'Sh'?" she asked.

"No, it's 'Ch'; don't worry, people have been getting it wrong my whole life."

The receptionist didn't look at all worried, as she replied, "No, I'm afraid it isn't coming up, sir."

Eddie was beginning to get annoyed. He leaned over the counter to get a glimpse of the monitor. Since the countertop was about four feet in the air and he was five-foot, six inches tall, this attempt forced him to stand on the toes of his pointed black shoes. His black slacks pulled up to reveal white sweat socks.

"I know he used to work here…"

"Not according to the computer. I don't have a 'Chandran' listed as having worked here or anywhere on this campus, for that matter."

"That just doesn't make sense," Eddie said, a frown crossing his dark face. He ran one hand through a shock of black hair, leaned back and bit his lip.

Realizing that he wasn't going away, the receptionist rolled her chair towards a metal door in the wall behind her desk that was framed just under a banner that read "Ulent Labs: Working to Save the World One Day at a Time." Without standing up, she pulled down on the door's handle, and yelled, "McAvitch, get out here! I've got a situation."

"No, no, there's no need for trouble," Eddie said as he backed up. "It's no trouble," the receptionist replied, as a tall, skinny kid burst out the door. "This is a public lab, paid for by your taxes. We're required to let the public see what we do—we just make sure you have a proper escort. McAvitch here will show you around—maybe this Chandran is a visiting scientist."

"Follow me," McAvitch said, gesturing towards the metal door. Reluctantly, Eddie did as he was told. He was a little curious to find out what was behind those doors. But, once on the other side, his curiosity turned to disappointment. It was just a series of cubicles in an open bay, around which ran doors to outer offices. From his vantage point, Eddie could see all sorts of women and men busily working at computer terminals or reading reports. "Over there, behind that door, is the situation room," McAvitch said pointing at a heavy oak door in the corner behind them. "We can monitor weather patterns using satellite imagery from any point of the globe. Right now, we've been watching the tsunami as it rolls back from the East Coast."

"I'd like to see that," Eddie said, as he walked towards the door. McAvitch put his hand on Eddie's shoulder. He pulled the shorter man to a stop. "Nope, you've got to have a security clearance to go anywhere in the outer layer."

"I guess I'll just assume my tax dollars are being put to good use back there," Eddie muttered as he removed McAvitch's hand from his shoulder. "Let's continue," McAvitch said, as he pointed towards another door. "That's our command post for volcanic activity—we have information coming in from observation posts on every mountain in the Cascade Range ... except for Mt. St. Helens, currently."

"Again, I'm sure the taxpayer's money is being put to good use back there," Eddie threw in, as McAvitch made no effort to open the door. "I suppose you yourself are paid quite a bit ..."

"No ... not a cent!" McAvitch twitched as he folded his arms across the chest of his Harvard sweatshirt. "We're all unpaid research assistants back here."

"Unpaid ... then why do you do this?"

"Are you kidding, this is what you've got to do if you want to earn your Ph.D. First, you TA in one of the freshmen survey courses, then you get to teach an upper-division course, then you're here, and finally, if you're lucky, you get to conduct ground-breaking research and write a report—under the name of your advising professor, of course—all so you can earn your Ph.D."

"You do all that for free..."

"No, not for free," McAvitch answered. "It has taken me nine years to get to this point, and I've already run up over a 100 grand in student loans."

"But then you'll be able to get a good job and start paying all that back?" Eddie asked innocently as he earnestly wanted to know how it worked.

"No, of course not; then you get to maybe teach at a community college ... or work your way up the ranks to an untenured position at a university where you write reports for someone else and manage their grad students, and, finally, if you're lucky, get into a tenure-track full professorship."

"So why do you do it?" Eddie persisted.

"Because this is science we're doing here. We're gaining new knowledge on the age-old problems. We're shattering old beliefs and superstitions. We're forging a new world…"

"And because, let me guess, after going through all of *this* hell, you want the chance to turn around and do the same to someone else … am I right?" Eddie joked.

McAvitch's response was entirely humorless, "I guess it's just something that people like you from outside of the scientific community aren't capable of understanding. We're part of something larger than ourselves. We're making breakthroughs here every day. We're going to cure cancer, stop the aging process, and wipe out famine and disease. We're doing all of the things that people used to pray to an imaginary god to try to make happen." Spurred on by the thought of his recent near-death experience, Eddie asked, "You people don't believe in God?"

"Of course not—although we sometimes joke that Ulent is god, the way they make us shape up every time he comes back to town to inspect the lab. God was just a convenient explanation for things that people didn't understand before Darwin came along. We now know that it's just survival of the species—each individual trying to…"

"But what's the point?"

"What do you mean, what's the point?"

"I mean, if there is no God, why go to all the trouble to survive? Why try to find out something new, why try to discover anything? Why prolong the agony of living? What's the use of adding to the body of knowledge, if it's just survival of the species? Why bother?"

"Because," McAvitch said with complete certainty, "It's what we do."

"Why not put the children to work in the fields and the mines again—wouldn't it be more efficient than letting them waste all of those years in school? What would make slavery wrong; no offense intended for this system you've got here, of course? What's to keep people from raping and killing? Why can't the strong just take what they want from the weak? How can there be anything good, any higher ideals to call upon, without God?"

McAvitch was becoming annoyed; his voice cracked as he answered, "If there was a god, why would it allow people to suffer and die? Why would it allow Crusades and Inquisitions in its name? ... Look, I don't have time to discuss junior high school philosophy with you. Can't you see? We're trying to save the world around here. We are following the lead of Dr. Ulent here. He's a genius!"

"If he's such a genius, how come he's not President of the United States?" Eddie asked clearly relishing the chance to needle his taller foe. "How come he's not greeted like a rock star when he comes to town—except for here? I've never even seen a picture of this guy in the newspaper..."

"Come over here," McAvitch angrily replied. "If that will make you shut up, I've got a picture in my office right here!"

"No," Eddie said, starting to walk away. "I don't need to see it ..."

"I've got it right here ... come on!" McAvitch waved Eddie towards a cubicle near the back door of the lab. Eddie reluctantly followed McAvitch over. As he did, the back door burst open, and a tall bearded man walked in. He brushed past Eddie. "Oh, there you are—I've been looking for you for the past hour," McAvtich called out to the bearded fellow. "Did you take care of those faxes as I asked?"

"Yeah, don't worry. They're all gone."

"Good," McAvitch said before turning his attention back to Eddie who was now standing beside him in the opening to the cubicle. There McAvitch pointed to the fuzzy wall of the cubicle. In a corner, taped up over the top of where a cot was set up, was a poster. The upper-left-hand corner of it had come loose. It was emblazoned with the words "Nobel Laureate" in the upper right-hand corner. In the center was the picture of a dark-haired man with black-rimmed glasses who was using his fists to prop up his angled chin. In the bottom left-hand corner it had been signed in black ink.

"That's who you're calling Ulent! That's your genius. ... That's your god?" Eddie said with astonishment, as he pointed towards the poster. A big smile spread across Eddie's face, "Oh, brother ... Now that's funny!"

·· ◆ ◆ ◆ ◆ ◆ ··

"Yes, I told you I'd bring it. I'm already at the mall—believe me; it wasn't easy to get my car downtown. Someone set up a bonfire right in the middle of Hawthorne Bridge.

...Yes, I remember, Game Wild. I knew you'd come back to me. ...Hello ..."

Ian put the cell phone back in the front pocket of his tan corduroy shorts. He had dressed to impress Anna; the rest of his outfit was comprised of a blue turtleneck sweater, white tube socks, tan sandals, and, to top it all off, a Panama hat with a white bandana wrapped around the middle. He had showered, brushed his teeth, cut his toenails, filed down his fingernails, and thrown on aftershave (although he hadn't actually shaved; he figured the fuzzy hairs on his face made him look more mature). He crossed the vacant street and made his way to the glass doors that led into the bottom level of the Pioneer Place Mall. He paused in front of the doors, where Statue Man was poised—still and silent—atop a small, wooden platform. For as long as Ian could remember, Statue Man had stood underneath this awning, at the northeast entrance to the mall, every Saturday. Normally, he was covered in silver paint, although today it was gold. As soon as a tourist dropped a coin in the pot in front of his platform, he would suddenly turn to shake their hand. This act often threw quite a scare into visitors to Portland. Seeing a paint-covered man suddenly move could be quite a shock. Statue Man had once been threatened with a lawsuit after a vacationer from the Netherlands nearly died of a heart attack—the whole case was settled out of court for an undisclosed amount, but a local newspaper had wagged that it was "likely a significant chunk of change".

Usually, Ian just walked past Statue Man; but today, with no one else around, he suddenly felt the need for companionship of any sort. He pulled a penny and two dimes out of his pocket, and threw them into the pot. Then he waited for Statue Man to reach down to shake his hand. But he didn't. Instead, he did something Ian had never witnessed before. Statue Man leaned down until his face was only inches from Ian's oversized ears. Ian could feel Statue Man's warm breath against the side of his face. He spoke. To be more exact, Statue Man whispered, "Act natural—they're watching us." Ian froze up and listened. "Whatever you do, don't go in there! There are people in there—crazy people; vampire people. I don't know what they are, but people go in and they don't come out. They smell fingers too." Then, Statue Man snapped back into position. Once more, he was a gold-covered man, standing still atop a rickety wood frame. Ian paused and tried to peer through the glass doors to the mall. But he didn't see anything.

I did promise Anna, he thought. *And besides, who takes the advice of a man who covers himself in paint for a living?*

So Ian did the very thing that he had always criticized characters in horror movies for doing: he walked into the mall after having been warned not to do so. The Statue Man continued to stand perfectly still.

At that very same moment, on the southwest side of the mall, Anna opened the glass doors to go in. But something made her stop in mid-stride with the door's gold-painted handle in her hand. She paused to listen. She could swear that she heard someone screaming. She looked to the left and then to the right. There was nothing.

She had now been awake for over 42 hours and already Anna was having trouble discerning reality from fiction. She figured this screaming was just another hallucination. She walked straight into the mall.

Ian headed down the brightly lit hall, loudly stomping over top of the tile floors. He looked in all the windows of the shops, in order to make sure that he saw nothing odd. *There ARE people in there,* he realized. *So everything must be OK. That Statue Man must have just gone berserk—probably been sniffing too much of his body paint or something.* Just to reassure himself, Ian walked into the first shop he came to, a Hap gender-neutral clothing store. He walked to the counter. The woman behind the counter didn't acknowledge his presence, she made no effort to make eye contact—*so far, all was normal.* He walked towards a display rack in the back of the store. A tall man, wearing a cheap blue blazer, followed him. *So I've got security following me—that's normal,* Ian thought. He walked out of the store and continued down the wide hallway. Pioneer Place hallways featured little lights in the floor that wove a path through the blue-green tile; Ian followed them. As he walked, he glanced through the windows of the shops that he passed—just to be on the safe side. But the more shops that he passed, the more uncomfortable he became. Something just wasn't right, after all.

He did an inventory of his sensations to try to figure out what was off. *Was it a sound? Was it the smell?* Ian arrived at the entrance to the Game Wild store. He didn't see Anna so he took a seat on a wooden bench across from the store and tried to sort it all out. As Ian watched the people in the stores, he realized what it was that was bothering him. All of a sudden, it was all too clear.

He heard the loud clicking sound of someone's heels striking the smooth surface of the floor and looked in the direction from which it came. A moment later, around from the corner, a woman's figure appeared. Ian started to stand up. But once the face came into view, he realized that this wasn't Anna.

The older woman, draped in a sundress and wearing sunglasses, made her way across the hall. She sat down right next to Ian on the bench. She pulled off her sunglasses and set them beside her. The woman had her eyes closed before Ian had a chance to make eye contact. Ian realized she must have fallen asleep. *Narcolepsy*, he thought. *I remember Anna reading something about that.* He turned his heavy body away from this new person and slid as far away from her on the bench as possible. Ian then tried to return to his thoughts. He was again interrupted when he heard a dull thudding sound echoing off the floor from around the corner. He looked up again. A young woman's form, dressed in a soiled sweatsuit, became visible. Ian had never noticed what she usually wore so he didn't realize it was Anna until her face appeared. She didn't smile exactly; in fact, it looked more like she grimaced as she approached—but Ian was happy for any hint of recognition. He sat on the bench and waited for Anna to reach him.

"Alright, I'll take whatever you've …" she began.

But Ian stuck a fat finger to his lips. He was staring across the hall at the shops.

"What are you looking at?" Anna exclaimed, her loud voice echoing up and down the hall.

The silver-haired woman, at the other end of the bench, snorted but didn't open her eyes. Ian leaned forward, to try to get a better look at what was happening in the store.

"Quiet!" he hissed. "They'll hear you."

"Who?" Anna whispered back, turning to try to figure out what Ian was looking at.

"I don't know—the ones that smell fingers, I guess," Ian whispered back, unaware of the perplexed look that Anna shot at him. "I went into Hap and the sales lady wouldn't help me."

"Yeah… So what? That's what always happens at Hap— they're stuck up."

"And a man dressed like security followed me…"

"They always do that—it's your ratty hair cut. You should go to a barber, you know that."

"No, I mean it. There's something wrong. Look at them—they're just kind of floating around. They aren't talking, they aren't looking at anything, they just keep circling…"

"It's the great American Pastime—it's called shopping…"

"OK, so then why do they all have new clothes?"

"Again, shopping…"

"No, I mean completely new clothes—with the tags still on?"

This was a little harder for Anna to answer. She tried to see what Ian was talking about, but her eyes were tired and everything looked hazy, the people looked yellow.

"I don't know… They're trying them on, I guess," she said, in her normal speaking voice, as she turned back to face Ian.

This time the woman at the other end of the bench awoke with a start at the sound of Anna's voice. She opened her eyes. Just then, the lights went black. The electricity had cut out. Ian, who was still peering through the dark at the windows of the shops, whispered, "Look—see, I'm telling you! There's something funny about their eyes."

"I know," Anna whispered in return as she backed away from the bench. She kept her eyes trained on the dark shape of the woman that sat near to Ian. It wasn't difficult to do, even in the dark. "Her eyes," she whispered as she pointed. "They're glowing—red!"

Ian turned to see what Anna was talking about. He screamed and jumped up from the bench. He went running towards the exit corridor. Realizing that he had left Anna alone—and that this probably wasn't the best idea if he wanted to win her back—Ian stopped once he reached the corner. He went running back to where Anna was standing. She was frozen in place. The old woman at the other end of the bench was trying to stand up but was having a tough time with it. It reminded Anna of when she had volunteered as a waitress for a "Parrot Head Margarita Night" at an old folk's home.

"Come on, let's get out of here!" Ian hissed, as he grabbed Anna's wrist and dragged her down the hall. "What happened to your sleeve, anyway? Did you spill soup on it or something?"

Before Anna could answer, the lights came back on. The moment they did, the old woman's eyes snapped back shut. She walked forward and straight into the pane of glass emblazoned with the words "Game Wild."

"Look—they've all gone back to circling," Ian whispered to Anna as the two of them slowly continued to sneak down the hall. The overhead lights flickered and then went dead again. This time the hallway filled with many tiny red glows. They emanated from every angle around Ian and Anna.

"They're swarming us!" Anna shrieked.

The old woman, her eyes opened, turned and grabbed hold of the sleeve of Ian's turtleneck and pulled his hand towards her face.

"Oh, no you don't!" Ian yelled as he balled up the fist of his other hand and slammed the old woman in the face. "You're not going to smell my fingers—you psycho!"

He grabbed Anna by the arm again and pushed through the crowd of red-eyed people that had gathered around them. They sprinted towards the end of the hall, the red glowing all around. Suddenly the lights came back on. Anna pulled Ian to a stop, trying to catch her breath. She glanced back—to make sure they were a safe distance away from their pursuers.

"Look…they've gone back to circling…with their eyes shut," Anna whispered as she gasped for breath, "It's the light." Then she added, "You knocked that old hag's jaw off!"

Ian looked back. Sure enough, the old woman was scraping the lower half of her jaw off of the floor and was trying to push the bloody mess back into place in her face. "Well, she had it coming. She didn't smell my fingers—she tried to bite me!" Ian said, turning away from the scene with a shudder. "Ewww—that's so gross. And I used to tell my Sobo I thought it was disgusting when she took her dentures off in public."

"What are these things?" Anna asked, the fingers of her hands intertwined behind the back of her head as she tried to get air into her lungs. "Where did they come from?"

The couple was now in the open-air portion of the mall. They stood near a wall that held the doors to one of the elevators. They could see every level of the east end of the mall above them. There didn't appear to be any movement. "I'd rather take my chances going up than across," Ian said, as he turned to press the "Up" button for the elevator. "We might as well take the easy way."

"Don't you think we should take those instead?" Anna asked as she pointed towards a door marked "Stairs" that stood nearby. "Bad things always happen in the elevator…"

"That only happens in the movies," Ian replied confidently.

Just then, the elevator bell rang out. The metal doors slowly slid apart and open. Anna's eyes opened wide. She grabbed hold of Ian's arm. The two of them slowly backed away from the elevator's opening. Two gaunt men with their eyes closed walked out of the elevator. They blindly walked straight towards Anna and Ian. They seemed to be sniffing the air. The bodies of these naked men—from head to toe—looked entirely deflated.

"See, I told you that all men have that problem from time to time," Ian whispered, as he pointed towards the men's bared waists—then he screamed, "Run!"

They sprinted back down the hall from which Ian had originally come, over the top of the sparkling lights in the blue-green tile. They could hear shuffling footsteps behind them the entire way. The shuffling grew louder as more of the gaunt bodies joined the chase. Just then, in front of them, another pack of yellowish people, in various stages of dress, appeared. Ian and Anna slid to a stop with Ian desperately looking around for another way out.

Seeing that Hap was now empty, Ian led Anna into it. They ran to the back of the store, to the well-lit changing area. Ian threw the entry door to the changing room shut and wedged a coat rack against it. Suddenly the rack began to rattle as bodies began to push against the door from the outside. Anna ducked into a changing booth. Ian followed her and closed the slatted dressing room door.

"Yeah, like that's going to hold them for long," Anna remarked as she fell to the carpeted floor. "Now what?"

"I don't know," Ian said, as he fell to the floor beside her. "What are those things?"

Ian propped up his elbows on his knees. He set his skull against the wide palms of his hands. Anna noticed that he must have lost his hat somewhere in the hallway while being chased. The rattling at the main door became louder. It sounded like more bodies were being thrown against it. Then, Ian looked up. A smile came to his face. "What are you smiling for?" Anna asked. "Because, I know what game we're playing," Ian said. "It's Ms. Pac Man ... remember—you and I used to play it all of the time."

"Yeah," Anna said, surprised that Ian had managed to remember this fact—and wondering why he had chosen this moment to walk down memory lane.

"The ghosts—they're not programmed very well. They're not smart!" Ian declared. Then he pointed up towards the ceiling, near the overhead lights. A narrow storage ledge ran from the end of the wall, behind them, to just over the doorway. "Oh, I get it," Anna said. "We can climb up there and ... but I don't think you'll fit…"

"No, I can't fit. Besides, I'm not the one who's trying to prove you can die from not sleeping," Ian said. "I'm not coming. Once the ghosts get in, they'll smell me over here. It will take them a while to figure out which booth I'm in and then a little longer to get through this door—because they're not smart. Hopefully, just like in Pac-Man, they'll all swarm to get me. You wait until the pack closes in and then hop down—and get out."

"No…there's got to be another way."

"There isn't, we're trapped here and we don't have much time." Ian stood up and pulled a folded packet of papers out of his back pocket. "This is the '51 Ways To End Your World' printout. Believe me, it was much harder to crack into this time. The other page is the one I found on Ulent's birth. The printer ink was running out so all that showed up was the top half—his home address, date of birth, and the city he was born in. Is Hyderabad in the Ukraine?"

"It must be—that's where the news said he was born," Anna answered as she pulled her cell phone out of the pocket of her hoodie before taking the papers Ian was handing her. As she did this, a folded-up piece of paper fell out of her pocket and to the ground.

"What's this?" Ian said as he grabbed the paper off of the floor. Anna replied, "Some guy gave that to me—he said it was from Ulent's lab. He said to look at the dates—it shows the detonation times for Ulent's nukes." Ian whistled as he sped read the paper, "This is important." Then he handed the page back to Anna. She stuffed all of the papers into her pocket. The door's rattling was steady now. "So you were right—Ulent is fucked up," Ian remarked as he grabbed Anna by the waist and lifted her towards the ceiling. "What do you mean?" she huffed back as she grabbed hold of the overhead shelf and slid onto it. "You didn't read it, did you?" Ian said. "That's always been your problem; if you were a character in a story it would be your fatal flaw."

"What's that supposed to mean?" Anna said.

"You never really plan ahead. It's the whole reason why you always wind up writing all your papers at the last minute—that's why you had to cheat and got thrown out of OPU, right?" Just then the door cracked open a sliver. Anna looked over the top of the booths and saw three hands pulling back at the cracked wood of the entry door. Then she saw purple shapes slithering up the changing room walls. She shrieked. "Oh my god! Now snakes are swarming us!" "Snakes!" Ian shrieked, even more shrilly. "Come on! What am I? Indiana Jones?"

"I've got to go now," Anna whispered as she pulled herself up toward the end of the shelf nearest the door. "Try to think positive. Don't worry, it's just a few blood-thirsty, red-eyed freaks … and some snakes. I'm sure it will all work out for you. I'll find help. You'll be fine."

"No, no … you'll never see me again. Besides, what does it matter? The world is ending, right? It's all shit anyway." Ian sat down in the back corner of the changing booth. He pulled his knees up toward his face. "Promise me something, Anna," he said, speaking loudly so as to be heard above the ripping of the door. "Promise me you'll do it right this time, that you'll go all the way. Read the papers and figure out how to stop that bastard from saving the world. *Whatever you do, don't let him save the world!*"

Anna dared not answer back from where she was perched on the shelf. The "ghosts" had broken in. Just as Ian said, they had begun to swarm in his direction. At least half a dozen of them blindly sniffed their way towards the booth where Ian hid. *At least the purple snakes seem to have disappeared*, Anna thought as she crawled along above it all on the shelf.

Ian looked up at Anna and saw that she was waiting for her chance to jump. He tried to smile at her but his face wasn't used to such displays. He heard the shuffling of feet and then saw those very same feet from underneath the slatted doorway to the changing room. Ian looked up again and saw Anna spring downward. He knew that meant the pack was upon him. *Don't leave me*, he thought, and then, *Go ahead, bitch, see if I care!* As he saw the door in front of him begin to shake, from the weight of multiple bodies pushing against it, Ian tried to think about other things. He thought about movies.

If this was a movie, I'd think this story was pretty cool. It is kind of original—first, we started with volcanic eruptions everywhere up and down the coast, and then suddenly we've got blood-sucking ghouls coming out of nowhere running around the mall. That's unique; in most movies, these creatures only show up after a … Oh, now I get it…that is a great plot twist, he thought to himself; but then the true horror movie critic in him kicked in. *No, I'd think it was lame. After all, there are always blood-sucking ghouls in these 'end of the world' movies. The writers really should think of a more original ending…* That was all that Ian had time to think as the slatted door broke open.

IV - Anna In Wonderland

"**S**o you made it out alive. Hurry up, get in!"

A camouflaged U.S. Army Humvee pulled up beside Anna as she ran in the middle of the street. The driver barked out the command in a high-pitched voice. Only moments before, Anna had just run out of the very same doors to the mall that she had originally entered. With some of the sniffing, red-eyed people still in pursuit, she had darted into the street. She looked through the passenger-side "window" (a sheet of plastic that was zipped down). Anna looked at the driver, a uniformed soldier with a nametag that read "Padgett." The driver looked through the window opening and back at the woman's face, which he hadn't clearly seen before. He saw that underneath close-cropped black hair, she had a slender face and green eyes. Her eyes were bloodshot and puffy. Ben realized that there was something familiar about her face. "Oh... I know you..." But before Ben could say anything more, a large hairy arm snaked around Anna's throat and began to tear her away from the side of the vehicle where she stood. Anna screamed and clawed at the olive green vinyl door. She used her fingers to clutch hold of the window's wire-framed opening, her fingernails digging into the vinyl.

Without thinking, Ben dove across the raised gear column set in the middle of the Humvee, grabbing hold of the black, plastic door handle, and twisting it open. All the while, Anna felt the life being choked out of her. Just as it seemed that her windpipe was about to break, she saw the soldier lean out of the Humvee and bite the arm that held her. She heard a howl as the arm let her loose and Anna felt herself pulled into the passenger seat. As more arms reached through the open passenger-side door to grab at Anna's body, Ben slid back into the driver's seat and pressed down on the gas. The Humvee accelerated down the street.

"Pull the door shut!" Ben ordered as a tall man leaped into the opening. A yellow-clad man was holding onto the vinyl top of the Humvee. He had one foot on the running board, with the other he kicked at Anna. She kicked back as Ben spun the vehicle around the corner. Anna's tennis shoe landed on the creature's knee and her next kick caught it in the chest. That, combined with the movement of the SUV, was enough to force the yellow-clad man to let go. It screamed as it fell onto the pavement and rolled out of sight.

Anna pulled the passenger door towards her side. It took her a second to figure out how to get the black handle to latch but she managed to get it to shut. She leaned back against the black, vinyl seat to try to catch her breathfeeling entirely exhausted. She then turned to look at the soldier who drove. "I didn't think I was going to make it," Anna said. "You really took a bite out of that thing."

"Yeah, well one good bite deserves another," Ben said with a chuckle as he stared straight ahead.

"What's that supposed to mean?"

"Nothing … You probably don't remember, but we've already met."

"I don't remember," Anna said as she reread the soldier's nametag. She looked at the pasty face of the dark-haired man who had rescued her, "'Padgett,' no, it doesn't ring a bell."

"Don't call me Padgett—people in the army don't have first names, and I'm not like them. Call me Ben."

"OK, Ben. I'm Anna—Anna Frod," then she smiled. Ben looked over at his passenger for the first time since she had gotten into his vehicle. He noticed her smile. "Is there something funny?" he asked. "Yes … no… Well, not funny-funny, but funny-sad. I was just thinking about this guy I met last night—and now I'm here, with you, a soldier. … Say, they didn't call you some sort of nickname when you were in high school, like 'Ben Gay' or anything like that. Because …" Ben cut Anna off with a glare. He rolled his eyes before turning back to face the road and beginning to speak. "Look, I don't know why you have a problem with me—all I've done today is to try to save your life twice…"

"Twice…just what are you talking about?"

"Lady, didn't you hear me screaming at you not to go into that mall? I've been sitting at that corner keeping people away from there for the past few hours—and you're the first one who just went barging in anyway. You must have a real problem with authority."

"You mean you saw me go in—and you didn't go in after me?"

"Look, it's kind of like when a plane goes down and they tell you to put on your oxygen mask before you help anyone else. I couldn't have done you any good out on that street if I'd been dead, now could I have? ...Besides, I had been ordered to keep an eye on those things until the rest of my unit could go in after them."

Some of Anna's anger from the night before was beginning to return, the skin on her cheeks flushing crimson, "Oh, and I'll bet you're real good at following orders. Especially when they include shooting into unarmed crowds..."

"Crowds that beat several soldiers and police—and I didn't exactly come out unscathed, let me tell you! How can you defend people who are fighting to get rid of all authority? How can you defend people who want to prevent scientists from doing their jobs? How can you possibly defend the actions of those who are fighting for the extinction of the human race?"

"Life is pain. People die every day! I should know...I watched a bullet rip through the skull of ...someone I met, last night, in Pioneer Square. And I just left my boyfriend in that mall..." Anna shoot back before faltering and changing her tone of voice. "Didn't you just say your unit was on the way to the mall? We can go back in and save Ian if he's still there... Where are we driving?"

They had just crossed the Broadway Bridge. Ben was turning onto ML King Way. It all looked so different in the ashen haze. "Change of orders," Ben said. "They were relayed to me just before you came out of the mall. My unit isn't coming back, they've given up on the city—it's in the hands of the rioters, looters, and God only knows what else those things were."

"Then he really is gone—Ian is really gone."

"I'm sorry for your loss. There's a whole world out there that's about to go up in flames if things don't happen quickly. A tornado just tore through Paris—they said nothing has devastated that city like it is now since … well since Napoleon or the blitzkrieg or something war-like. Anyway, freak weather is happening all over the place and the next big set of eruptions is due to hit. We've been ordered back to the armory in case Ulent needs us."

"Ulent—oh, what have I been thinking?" Anna asked as she pulled the papers out of the pocket of her sweatshirt jacket. "Look, can you drop me off at …let's see… 12513 Stafford Road—it's in Lake Oswego."

"12513 Stafford Road—is that your home address or something?"

"…Something like that," Anna mumbled as she put the papers back in her pocket and then snuck a look at the time on her cell phone.

"Hmm… That's an odd request," Ben mused, as he took another sidelong glance at the woman in the sweatsuit who rode with him. "I guess I can do that. It's sort of on the way, I suppose."

"Good," Anna said as she sighed and leaned back in the seat. Anna had now been awake for 43 hours and 17 minutes. In a few minutes, she hoped she would face Dr. Ulent. She had no idea what to expect when she did.

Then she pointed up at the dark sky. "Those floating balloon cartoon people are so pretty. They must be getting Portland ready for a parade." Ben scowled as he tried to look up in the direction Anna was dreamily staring. "I don't see any balloons." "Oh, they're so wonderful! I love the Garfield one, and the Papa Smurf. They add a nice touch of color to the clouds of ash." Ben tried once more craning his neck that direction, then gave up. "Probably some sort of terrorist scheme. I wouldn't trust anybody or anything right now—especially cartoon balloons." He was silent a moment, then added, "Cartoons, that's how they infiltrate countries you know. First, you start watching cartoons, then, next thing you know, you belong to a subversive organization." Anna sat frozen in her smile, her eyes glued to the sky. Ben muttered to himself, "I did always like G.I. Joe, though."

···◆◆◆◆···

"Yes, papa, I expect it's all OK. …No, I didn't see him, exactly.

I went to the university, just like you asked. Well, he doesn't work there anymore. …But I wouldn't worry.

…No, believe me, you mustn't worry. Did you hear back from all the others?

…Willie, too? …That's good, papa. Don't worry.

…No, don't watch the news. It will just upset you. …Yes, you're right—they should show more of the good things that are happening.

Just lie back in your bed. I'll be home to take care of you, soon.

I'd have been there already, but they've got all of the outgoing roads backed up, in pretty much every direction. People just don't know which way to run.

…But I know now, papa, I know where I am going. I'm going home. I'm coming home."

···◆◆◆◆···

"Let's ask for directions…"

"No," Anna insisted. "If you just keep going left, once we're across the bridge…"

"I'd rather stop and ask for directions," Ben replied.

"You know what you sound like right now?" Anna asked. "I thought it was always the woman who wanted to ask for directions." Ben slammed on the brakes forcing the Humvee to lurch forward. Anna threw up her arms in front of herself to keep her head from hitting the windshield. "Now listen here," Ben raged. "I've been with you for all of 30 minutes and you've done nothing but give out opinions about me, from my uniform to my sexual preferences. You just keep casting aspersions at me, labeling me with … well, some sort of scarlet letter. All you've done so far is to judge me by what you see, on the surface! How would you like it if I judged you by your clothes or your haircut? What if I judged you by your name?" That last point stung. Especially in light of what Dick had told Anna the night before, about how he had been made fun of because of his name— Anna could almost see his smiling face framed against the black sky, as she gazed off in the distance. "You're right," she quietly acknowledged.

"You're damn straight I'm right." Ben continued. "If you got to know me you'd realize there's a lot more to me than this uniform…"

"No, I meant you're right," Anna broke in. "We should ask for directions. Look, over there!" They were at the east end of Sellwood Bridge. Just below them, off to the left, cars and people were jammed into the parking lot of Okies Amusement Park. "We can ask for directions there."

"Fine," Ben answered as he started the Humvee forward again. He pulled up towards a group of men who were surrounded by empty beer cans at the edge of the parking lot. They were standing on top of a long furrow of dirt that separated the cars from the brightly lit amusement park. They had bags of golf clubs sitting beside them. "Why don't you get out here and ask these guys for directions."

Anna did just that. As she walked up towards them, she saw them draw clubs out of their bags. She heard what they were saying: "Alright, let's try for that convertible Mercedes over there—the red one, with the personalized license plate—'Zag'. The first ball in the back seat wins." The men dropped golf balls onto the ground in front of them preparing to swing.

"Excuse me," she said. The men ignored her. A heavy-set man drew his club upwards into his backswing. Much more loudly now, Anna said, "I said, 'Excuse me.'" The fat man's club hit the ball with a glancing blow. The white ball flopped forward three feet and came to rest in a red cooler nearby. "Nice shot, Sergio. It looks like you're ready for the tour!" one of the men called out. The hefty man whirled around to face Anna. He pointed down at her. "It was her. She said something while I was about to swing. That's a clear violation of course etiquette."

"You bet it is," one of the other men chimed in. "And we all know what the punishment is."

"We sure do!" one of the other men called out. "The first one to hit the bonny lass smack in the head gets to run for the next round ... or something like that..." The men all dropped their golf balls and turned brandishing their clubs. Anna started to back away. "I'm not aiming for her head." the fat man who had originally pointed out Anna's rules violation to the other judges declared. "I'm going for her bony little ass." Anna stood there, unsure of what to do. The hours of staying awake seemed to be catching up to her reflexes. "Run!" Ben yelled, as he grabbed hold of Anna and pulled her along, a hail of white balls raining down around the pair. A man's voice rang out behind them, "Reload!"

A stone archway sporting dark metal letters loomed ahead. The letters spelled out "Okies Amusement Park, EST. 1911." Ben and Anna rushed under this arch. They kept running past the empty ticket booth. They didn't stop until they were well inside the crowded park. There they leaned against the wooden frame of the bumper cars building. Anna furtively looked around her surroundings while she caught her breath. "That's odd," she pointed out to Ben. "There aren't any kids; these are all adults."

"Yeah," Ben agreed. "Most of the law-abiding families are probably staying in their homes as the President ordered. We've had reports of nothing but trouble makers on the streets." He paused and then added, "No offense." Anna ignored him and walked around the corner of the building where they had been resting to get a glimpse of what was going on inside. She looked through an open bay of the building. "Come, look at this," she hissed at Ben. Reluctantly Ben followed her and looked into the bumper cars' pit. Men and women—most looking like they hadn't had a sober moment in several hours—chased each other around in their little cars. Drunkenly they steered directly at the other drivers, loud cheers greeting each new pileup. As they passed by each other, the drivers slashed out at each other with their fingernails and fists. Several of them appeared to have been at this for some time, their faces covered in cuts. Blood was being spread by the rubber bases of the cars as they moved around on the smooth wood floor. Ben couldn't take his eyes off of the proceedings. Finally, Anna grabbed him by the arm, pulling him away. "Something is going on over there," she exclaimed as she pointed towards the crowd at the base of the Twirl-a-Hurl. As they walked towards the ride, Ben could smell the popcorn and cotton candy. He looked in the direction of the smell and saw that the concession stand doors had been broken. Inside people were greedily gobbling down the salty and sweet treats, the concrete around the stand littered with empty wrappers and cardboard boxes.

Anna looked ahead toward the door to the roller-skating rink. There a man stood with plastic bags hanging from his hands. As people passed him to go into the white clapboard building he scooped the bags into a large barrel at his side. Then he handed a bag to each person, before allowing them to pass. Anna squinted to see what he was putting into the bags. It looked like an assortment of pills—of all sizes and colors—were being distributed.

Loud rock music blared out of speakers that hung on poles throughout the park. At the moment, it was REM's version of the end of the world.

The Twirl-a-Hurl lifted riders high in the sky, a crowd gathered below it, watching it spin. The people below hurled insults at the riders who were all a blur high above. Suddenly, some sort of thick liquid poured down on the ground, the source one of the Twirl-a-Hurl riders. The multi-colored moisture splattered to the ground, mixing with the stains already in the cement. The crowd cheered loudly.

The ride operator in a nearby booth slowly lowered the circular platform to the ground. There it stopped spinning and a pale-faced woman with a soaked blouse lowered herself out of a metal harness and crawled towards the exit. One of her fellow riders, a heavy-set woman who had been standing upright beside her, stepped out of her harness to kick the woman causing the crowd to yelp in delight. The fat woman kicked her again and the woman on the ground rolled onto the moist concrete with a thud. The gathered onlookers went wild. The fat woman raised her fists in the air, the flabby skin under her arms shaking in waves.

As she went to return to her place, the heavy woman slipped on the slick metal surface and tumbled out of the opening to the ride. She landed on top of the other woman who was lying motionless on the pavement, blood spurting out of the prone woman's oversized nose. Again, the crowd broke out into another round of cheers. Above them, the booming voice of the ride operator overpowered the music through the speakers, "Ladies and gents, it looks like we have two openings, instead of one. All you have to do is throw all of your money into the pile we got going down here at the booth. Whoever lasts the longest without losing their lungs, will get to collect it all. Assuming the next eruption doesn't take us all out first, that is! We got at least seven hundred bucks here, folks! So try your luck on the Twirl-a-Hurl, just step right up!"

The heads on several of the riders lolled about lifelessly. It looked as if the metal harness was the only thing holding one or two of them in place. A crush of people moved to get onto the ride, but a burly man in a leather jacket pushed all but two giggling teenagers back. He ran his thick hands over their bodies as he locked them into place on the ride. The crowd cheered as the leather-jacketed man stepped back off the circular metal platform. The ride began to spin while it lifted into the air once more.

Anna was feeling sick from the stench of sweat and vomit. She pushed against Ben's uniformed chest. "We need to get out of here!" she pleaded. Ben led her towards the front of a brown building that stood nearby. The facade was made out of a metal piece that featured two trees, complete with birds and nests, and a brown guard rail. On the other side of the rail, carts rolled by on a track. Over the top of the gate that led into the ride, there was a banner that read, "Funhouse."

"Oh, I used to love this when I was a kid," Anna said, as she pushed through the crowds to get to the gate where empty carts emerged out of the darkness. There people eagerly jumped into them. "Come right in for the ride of your life— the only ride that matters!" the operator announced and then added. "It can last a minute, or it can last for hours; you never know."

"We have to try this!" Anna squealed, pulling Ben along with her. She pulled herself onto the front bench of one of the carts. Reluctantly Ben slid in beside her.

A middle-aged man and woman got onto the backbench of the cart and immediately began to caress each other. Ben watched the pair out of the corner of his eye as the cart began to move. The cart carried Ben and Anna from the dark of the ash-covered day into the pitch dark of the interior of the funhouse. Just before the cart moved into the belly of the building, Ben noticed that a packet of paper had fallen out of Anna's sweatshirt pocket. He picked it up and shoved it into the vest pocket of his camouflaged jacket. Then it was dark all around them. As the cart moved deeper into the building, the sounds of the crowds and the music blaring from the speaker disappeared.

The heat was overwhelming in this tunnel. Ben could feel the sweat breaking out from around his neck. He unbuttoned his jacket. Anna heard what sounded like drum beats. This was very different from what she remembered from when she was a little girl. The beats grew louder as the cart rolled through the stifling heat and darkness. She thought she could hear groans and squeals mixed in with the drums. Then the cart lurched to a stop. Ben thought he felt a pair of hands on the back of his head. He turned to bark at the couple that had been riding behind him and Anna but it was too dark to see anything. He felt more hands pulling at him from all directions. He reached around in the darkness for the cart's metal bar and grabbed hold of it. "Ben, is that you? Are you still here?" he heard Anna say. Her voice floated back to him from some distance away. He realized that she had been pulled out of the other side of the cart. Without a moment's thought, Ben let go of the bar and let the hands pull him away. Without him in it, he heard the cart start up again and roll away.

There were bodies all around him, fingers feeling for him from every direction. He felt the crush of them against him in the darkness, gyrating to the steady beat of the drum. Anna felt hands slipping under her jacket, pulling it down. She felt fingers groping between her legs, the moaning getting louder. Ben threw out his hands in the darkness as he stumbled forward, his palms brushing against an uncovered nipple—which with his limited experience, he wasn't sure if it was male or female. Anna felt the warm skin of a naked body moving against her face. A woman's breast slowly brushed over the top of her lips and then her forehead. Ben felt a tongue work its way down his cheek and towards his chin. He didn't resist as the tongue moved over his lips and then into his mouth. He kissed back, his hands moving along the bare back of his unknown partner and then down across the strong hips. He pushed his pelvis against the bulge in the midsection of the body. Fingers felt along Ben's chest. He felt other hands against his thighs, moving up towards his waist. At least three hands worked to loosen the brass buckle that held up his camouflaged pants. Anna felt a pair of hands work their way over the waistband of her sweat pants and past her panties. She felt the fingers moving over the skin between her thighs. Suddenly, a long fingernail ripped into her skin, pain shooting through her as the hand forced itself upward. Anna tried to push away from the hand. It wouldn't let go. She screamed.

Anna's yell pulled Ben out of his sexual experimentation. He pulled away from the crush of the bodies and turned in the direction of her scream. Anna kept yelling until Ben stumbled against her. She only stopped when she heard his voice. "Anna—is that you?" Ben yelled, trying to be heard above the groans of ecstasy and the drums. "Yes!" Anna hissed back. She felt his hands against her shoulders and then over her chest. Ben moved his hands to her face once he realized what he'd done. Emboldened by his presence, Anna kicked against the body in front of her. She heard a snarl as the hand moved out from between her thighs. "Let's get out of here!" Anna hissed. "Yes," Ben replied. Ben's hand moved down her arm. Anna took his hand in hers. They stumbled through the darkness, moving away from the sounds of the drums and sex.

Ben used his boots to feel along the ground for the steel track upon which the carts ran. Presently, he struck it with his toe. Moments later, Ben and Anna were onboard a passing empty cart. As it moved through the darkness, they silently adjusted their clothing. They pulled out of the funhouse and into the ashy light of the afternoon. They were the only exiting occupants on a series of carts that were lining up to take on new passengers.

Anna ran towards the front gate—past the "Hall of Mirrors"—and Ben followed. Anna threw herself into one of the beds of flowers that lined the amusement park's walkway. She stared up at the dark sky. Ben didn't know what to do or say. He wasn't sure if he felt shame or regret. He just stood there, looking down at Anna's motionless body.

Then, he remembered the paper she had dropped in the cart. He pulled the pages out of the pocket of his jacket, unfolded the first one, and began to read. The title was "51 Ways To End Your World." As he stood there and read, Ben became light-headed, his world beginning to spin. He sat down on the ground next to Anna, then he laid down next to her, the two of them silently observing the dark clouds overhead, lost in their thoughts.

"That damned woolly mammoth doesn't deserve a piece of the pie!" Anna broke the silence to declare. "What do you mean?" Ben demanded, sitting up. "What do you mean?" Anna returned, also sitting up to eye him suspiciously. Ben looked back at her quizzically. They both stared at each other for the better part of a minute. Then they broke eye contact and fell into a thoughtful silence once more. They both laid back in the flower bed.

Finally, Ben had made his decision. He sat up, his voice filled with conviction, as he lay the packet of papers next to her and said, "These are yours. I can't say I understand it all, but it looks like Ulent is making a big mistake." Anna stared straight up. Her head didn't move. Only her chest's steady movement—up and down—let Ben know she was still alive. "Come on, we've got to hurry if we are going to stop them," he said. These words roused Anna from her trance and she sat up, before picking up the papers. "We? ... Why the sudden change of heart?" Anna asked. "Maybe you're right, that there isn't anything worth saving. Look around us—look at what we've become. All along I thought that maybe there was something deep down, something good in everyone—in me and us all. ... But I was wrong—I was naive. I know better now. This here is all we are and nothing more...," Ben said as he looked down at his boots. For reasons he didn't understand and couldn't quite explain, he didn't want to look into Anna's eyes. Anna lifted her tired body to a standing position as she said, "But we still don't know how to get to Dr. Ulent's house. We still have to get directions..."

"There's a lot about me you don't know." Ben cut in. "I know exactly how to get to his house. I know that address—I've known it the whole time. But we've got to hurry if we're going to stop Ulent from saving the world."

V

*A*t that exact same amount, on the very same earth, the following events occurred:

A gibbon screeched to signal to its kin that an intruder approached.

Geese dove to escape the downpour of hail.

Three fish were simultaneously sucked into the belly of a whale. A torn piece of seaweed joined them.

Drying worms lay across the pavement after a rain storm.

A frog unrolled its tongue to catch a fly.

A cedar tree fell in the forest. Its plunge crushed an empty nest. Nobody knows for sure if it made a sound.

An eagle lifted its wings and stretched out its talons. Far below, a rabbit, already bleeding from the ear, froze in place.

Leaves circled the eye of a tornado.

A sand crystal, formed at the bottom of the sea, was churned ashore by a wave.

Bass leaped for gnats that swarmed over the surface of a lake.

A sleeping dog broke wind.

The wind howled.
Raccoons mated.
A dolphin smiled.

··✦✦✦✦✦··

"Here it is," Ben said as he stooped down to lift a corner of a brown mat. He stood up with a key in his hand. He inserted the key into the lock of a large green door that stood in front of him. "Come on in," Ben said as he started through the front door of the large colonial-style house. "It doesn't look like anyone is home. They're probably stuck out on some highway, trying to escape." Anna hesitated on the cement steps that led into the suburban house, and said, "But this isn't 12513 Stafford."

"No, but it is 12514 William Lane," Ben answered. "This is my old house. Trust me; you'll want to see this."

Anna figured it was worth taking a chance with this soldier. After all, Ben had already saved her life at least twice. "OK, I guess you're not going to try to turn me over to the authorities or anything else." Ben stared back at the dark-haired woman. The skin of his brow, underneath his ash-covered hair, furled into rows. He bit his lip. "No, I'm not going to turn you over to the proper authorities."

He walked in over the top of a Persian rug in the hallway and then turned to go up a narrow carpet-covered staircase. He had taken off his camouflaged jacket during the ride south from Sellwood to Lake Oswego. Now he wore only his brown standard-issue army t-shirt tucked into his field pants. As she followed him Anna noticed that he had missed a loop in the back of the waist of his pants with his cloth black belt.

"You're going to see something special—up here, in what used to be my bedroom."

"I bet you promised a lot of girls they'd see something special in your bedroom. …Back when you were in high school, I mean."

Ben stopped at the top of the staircase and looked down at Anna, his eyes looking directly into hers. "No—never, not once," he said, very earnestly. "It's right over here." He turned and walked into a room just off the top of the stairway. Anna walked in after him and looked around. The centerpiece of the room was a child's bed covered in a Star Traders blanket. Toy cars and rockets were strewn about the plush carpeted floor. The walls were painted to feature Star Traders cartoon characters. "So, you were a big Star Traders fan. I am learning something about you," Anna said with a smile as she fell backward onto the plush mattress. "Did you have the matching pajamas?"

Ben stepped back from the edge of the bed. He moved towards a side window. "No, I told you, this used to be my room. I moved out three years ago, right after I joined the Army National Guard. My parents live in Lincoln City now. I don't even know who owns this house now—we're just lucky we found the key."

"So what did you want to show me then?" Anna asked, as she sat up and moved her tired body to sit at the edge of the bed. "I'll tell you in a second," Ben answered, as he looked out the window. "You know, you've never mentioned your parents. Aren't you worried at all about them?"

"I don't even know them," Anna replied as she scratched her chin with her index finger. Ben saw that this left a black smudge right beneath her bottom lip. Anna closed her eyes. "I know I had parents, once. I lived with my grandmother for a while. Then I had foster parents—that didn't…well, let's just say that didn't end well. I ran away when I was 14, did a bunch of stuff that didn't work out well, started attending school at the New Directions for Youth Center with the other homeless kids in downtown Portland, and that's how I wound up getting accepted to OPU."

"So you made something of yourself; pulled yourself up by your bootstraps and all of that."

"Yeah, something like that," Anna said without looking at Ben. She quickly changed the subject as she turned back to face him, "So how'd you end up in the army—it doesn't look like you needed the money. This isn't exactly a lower-class neighborhood."

"My dad was in the army, during the first Gulf War. I just want … well … I wanted to do something to give back to my country as he did. …It hasn't been what I expected." Ben took a step towards Anna. He sat down on the edge of the bed beside her. "Listen," he said. "There's something I have to tell you." Anna turned to face him, sitting there, on the edge of some kid's bed, as they were just inches from each other. Anna could smell his musky body. Ben swallowed hard. He placed his palms on either side of his face, brought them together over his mouth, and sighed.

"I already turned you in—while we were at the amusement park. When I had you ask for directions, I radioed in that I'd caught one of the terrorists from the Pioneer Place protest."

Anna jumped up off of the edge of the bed. She stamped her foot. She clenched her fists. "Then it's all over!" she yelled.

She unclenched her fist and slapped Ben across the face, hard. The snap of her hand left a red mark on his cheek.

Ben stood up. He took a step towards Anna. "You only pretended to help me, this whole time? No wonder you took the woolly mammoth's side. …Don't come near me. It's all over. You've ruined it all." Anna spat out, as she pushed against Ben's chest with both of her hands. Ben grabbed her arms. He pulled her towards the window. "No, it's not over. That's why we are here. I *am* helping you! They ordered me to bring you into the armory, to turn you over to the MPs—but instead we're here. Don't you see?" he asked as he took one of his hands off of her struggling body to point at something out the window. Anna looked out the window. Across the back yard, she saw another colonial house, kitty-corner to the one in which she stood. It was surrounded by a tall, cement fence, the top of which was covered in broken glass and razor wire. "What is it?" she asked suspiciously as she stopped pushing to escape from Ben's grip. "I told you, I knew that address from the moment you said it. I was raised right behind it. We used to hit baseballs over the fence and then we'd have to crawl through that culvert—over there—to get them. It begins behind that ridge and ends in a drainpipe behind his shed. I haven't been able to fit through it since I was 11, but you should be able to make it. I'm telling you, that's 12513 Stafford Road."

Anna looked up into Ben's face. She looked right into his eyes to judge if she could trust him. He let her arms go. Wearily she let them fall to her side and took a deep breath. "I have to trust you. There's no one else to trust. I don't have anyone left. I need to trust you; I need to believe you."

Ben cupped Anna's chin in his left hand. He used his thumb to try to wipe away a black smudge. He moved his hand away from her face. "You can trust me; you can believe me. I've gone AWOL for you. I've disobeyed a direct order. I've stolen a military Humvee—I've broken into a house," Ben said looking straight into Anna's eyes as he spoke. "I'm ready to help you do the right thing. Together we can end this world."

"That is his Lake Oswego home right over there," he added. "That is Dr. Ulent's house."

···✦✦✦✦···

Just as Ben had said, it was a tight fit, but Anna was able to squeeze in through the pipe. She had to push through a cover at the end of it and then, caked in dirt, she walked up toward the house. She stopped when she reached the back door. She turned to look up at the window of Ben's house where he had promised to keep an eye out for her. Anna couldn't be sure, but she thought she saw his shadow. Somehow, seeing that shape made Anna feel like she wasn't so alone. She took the cell phone out of her pocket to check the time. It was 4:07 pm, Saturday afternoon. Anna had been up for 49 hours and 2 minutes. *Wouldn't it be funny if he wasn't here*, she thought. *Well, not funny as much as pathetic. In fact, what are the odds that he's here— after all, he's got two or three labs and his work in Washington D.C. ... Maybe this is just stupid.* She knocked anyway. She shivered as she waited there in the gritty afternoon haze on Dr. Ulent's back patio. She went to put away her cell phone. As she put her hand in the pocket, she felt the crumpled wad of papers. The moment she felt them, a wave of regret surged through

Anna. *I didn't read them—I didn't read the papers. The last thing Ian asked me to do and I didn't get it done.* It was too late now. She heard footsteps and then the door pulled open.

"Don't Girl Scouts normally come to the front door?" a dark-haired, dark-skinned man leaned out of the doorway to ask. "Are you the Dr. Ulent?" Anna asked, her words coming out more quickly than she'd intended. It seemed to take the clean-shaven man a moment to comprehend the question. His uni-brow twisted down towards his nose, driven by the wrinkles in his forehead. The middle-aged man's lips clenched together and he started to shut the door, "Sorry—no time for visitors."

"Not so fast," Anna insisted, as she wedged her foot in the door. "I need to talk to you about the 51 ways to end the world." There was a pause and then the door swung back open. The man stepped aside and let her pass, "Well then, come on in." Anna walked into the darkened hallway and waited. The man closed the back door and brushed past her as he continued forward. Anna assumed she was to follow. She noticed that the man seemed to be wearing a silk pajama top tucked into gray slacks. His feet were bare and padded softly over the wood floor. He walked past the bottom of a stairway. It seemed to Anna that the staircase was positioned exactly in the same place as they had been in Ben's old house next door.

He continued into a room that was brightly lit by lamps—all the curtains were drawn shut. He gestured for Anna to sit on a suede couch set against the far wall on the other side of a glass coffee table. "Go ahead, sit down," he said as he dropped into a thick wooden chair next to a roll-top desk. Anna did as she was told. The cushions were soft and she sank into them.

Suddenly Anna realized just how tired she was and she rubbed her eyes.

"You don't realize it but you've just made your first mistake," the man said as he lifted the roll-top and took out a plate that held a cream-covered piece of pie with a cherry on the top. "Now, I've got this, to keep the conversation honest. Don't let this be your last mistake."

Anna wondered what he meant by her "last mistake." Even more curious, however, was the fact that he kept a piece of pie in his desk.

"Now," he said. "Just exactly what do you have to say to me?"

Anna realized that she had no idea what was she going to say or do next. She had been so busy trying to get to Dr. Ulent's house that she hadn't had time to think about how she would stop him from saving the world once she got there. *It isn't like I could sneak up behind him and hit him over the head—he already knows I'm here. Maybe I could pretend like I have a gun in my pocket, and then take him hostage. But what if he demanded to see my gun? Maybe Bindi was right—just leave a strongly worded note.* As she tried to sort out a solution in her mind, she blurted out, "As I said, I found your report, the one called '51 Ways To End Your World' on the Internet. It was easy to hack into—that wasn't too smart, now was it, Dr. Ulent?"

As long as she had no idea what she was talking about, Anna figured it was best to sound confident about what she said. It was sort of like delivering a presentation in one of her classes—even if everything you said was bullshit, they gave you good grades if you sounded sure of yourself. Dr. Ulent seemed to be buying it. He pursed his lips together again before replying.

"That Scrodtop—I knew the government security systems were no good. So you know everything, then?"

"I sure do," Anna said.

"Well, it looks like you're a little smarter than I originally figured."

Anna didn't think this was much of a compliment. She leaned back and tried to look like a smart, confident person. In short, she did her best imitation of Ian Takki. "Yeah, that's right. It looks like we have something to talk over now, doesn't it, Oppenheimer?"

"Call me Op…"

"Doc Opulent?" Anna asked, incredulous.

"Just Op, please… Otherwise, I sound like a cartoon character. That must be exactly what you think of me—that I'm some sort of comic book villain. Yeah, if this was a trashy novel, they'd portray me in the dark shadows—up until the final act when I'd emerge as pure evil…"

"Well, that's just about the size of it, now isn't it?" Anna asked as she put one of her hands in the pocket of her sweat-shirt and tugged on the end of the papers. As she'd started doing her Ian impression, it suddenly came to her. She realized that she had only one way out of this jam. Ian had been right: Anna always did everything at the last minute; she never planned ahead. But now, those last-minute skills could come in handy. She would cheat her way past this scientific genius, this man who presidents came to for advice, and Anna would perpetuate the greatest scam of her life. It was as if she had suddenly realized what her purpose was in life. All of her school experiences had been preparing Anna to cheat the system. They had promised to prepare her for the real world, and now, here in Dr. Oppenheimer Ulent's living room, she was in it. "You're using nukes to control the earth—of course, you're evil."

"You'd better watch your mouth!" Ulent shot back, as he jumped to his feet.

He eyed the pie, as he continued, "That was a necessary evil. Don't you see? Sometimes in life, you have to do things which look bad on the surface, so that a greater good can come from it—for all humanity."

With Ulent standing, he turned to face the desk, while Anna slipped the papers out of her hoodie pocket. She placed them behind one of Ulent's oversized couch pillows. She was quietly trying to unfold them when Ulent turned back in her direction. "What if you needed prescription drugs to save your grandma's life—there wouldn't be anything wrong with stealing them, right? Or if you could go back in time, wouldn't you kill Hitler as a child so that he could never grow up to gas the Jews?" He asked looking directly at Anna. His eyes pleading for any hint of understanding.

"That probe you sent into Mt. St. Helens last month—and the explosion that killed the scientists..." Anna stammered as she looked for a way to complete her sentence. She was trying to buy some time so that she could scan the papers without Ulent catching her. "That was part of it, right?"

"Of course," he shot back, caught Anna off-guard, as she sucked in her breath. "Really?" she asked before realizing how this undercut the confident look she had going. "I just didn't think you'd admit to it," she added quickly. "Admit to it—why I'm proud of what I did. Those scientists knew the score. We needed a larger federal grant so we could do some real good by setting up an early eruption detection system in the Cascade Mountain Range. Haven't the last few days illustrated how necessary that is?"

"I guess."

"Well, you know everything, so you know... Well, it still shows what I mean... Anyway, congress wouldn't give us the money, so we used a standard academic procedure—we cooked some research, just a little bit." As Ulent spoke, a television screen descended in front of the staccato wall behind his head. Anna watched as a diamond-shaped submarine came onto the screen and was slowly lowered into a crater. "Everything went as planned, in the beginning. We had the scientists—Jenkins, Serengetti, and Captain Frieda—step into the submersible while the news crews were watching. Then we got them out of there—we hired a magician to help us accomplish that. We figured the titanium outer layer could withstand a few hours in the lava, but the pressure would have killed any people for sure. We ran a few hours of videotape from a sound stage up in Seattle, with the crew looking out windows while boiling hot lava flowed around them—it was some production!" As he continued, the screen behind him changed. The crumpled and steaming submersible was pulled out of the crater while the stunned news crews looked on. "We knew it couldn't hold humans, but we didn't think it would just collapse like that. We had to cover our tracks!" Anna stared at Dr. Ulent. She couldn't believe what she was hearing.

"Don't look at me like that. I did what had to be done; I did it myself. We couldn't have the scientists just show up alive after something like that—the retrieval was carried live on television all around the world. Would you rather that I let Scrodtop have all of the journalists killed as he wanted? I minimized the loss of life." Anna's knees began to shake. She realized she was in way over her head. This guy was no school teacher. "I told him a freak eruption that wiped out everyone who witnessed the submersible wouldn't cut it. The video had already gone out live via satellite. I explained it to our submersible crew. They were all scientists; they might have wept a little, but they understood. I put the gun to each one of their heads—they didn't beg for their lives; they knew it was no use. They went out like heroes. Frieda even grabbed my hand to hold it one last time—look; you can still see the marks!" Ulent exclaimed as held out the back of his left hand for Anna to see. Even from across the room she could see the long scabs running across the back of his hand and up past his wrist.

Oppenheimer turned away from Anna. He appeared to be wiping tears from his eyes and seemed shaken. Emboldened by this, Anna took another look at the top page she had hidden behind the cushion. She read as many words as possible before he turned back around. "So this massive chain of eruptions—number 14—it was just another item on your list. Just another ..."

"Yes, a fairly easy matter. There was a congressional investigation underway; I was about to lose my job. Scrodtop had lost the confidence of the president. We needed to make it right. ...We had to get hold of 10 nuclear weapons, but those have been floating around pretty freely ever since the Soviet Union broke up..." As he talked, Ulent paced. This allowed Anna to shuffle the papers and sneak a look at the one she had been handed by the bearded man on the OPU campus. "And that's why the nuke detonation dates were so important—they've already gone off. That was what really happened yesterday!" she exclaimed.

She was happy that she had finally figured out what had made this page so interesting to both Ian and Ben. Then she realized what this meant. The smile left her face. Her mind tried to grasp the dimensions of what she was now confronted with. "That means you killed all of those people ... my teacher's family ... all of the rest."

"Killed, no... that's too strong a word. Accidents happen when you do scientific research. There are unfortunate by-products. You can't make an omelet without breaking a few eggs."

While he spoke the faces of the dead flashed onto the screen. Ulent paced in front of it without noticing the crusted bodies, poking out of the lava, which appeared on screen. He wasn't aware of the black-smudged, burnt faces—faces of men, women, and children. "Besides, it wasn't my fault. I didn't miscalculate. Scrodtop's men couldn't get the nuke positioned on Mt. Rainier on time, so they just detonated two of them in the Mt. St. Helens crater, instead. The fools must have breached an unexpected pool of magma! Who can know for sure if all that lava wasn't already working its way to the surface? No one could have expected a reaction like that—maybe it was ready to blow on its own. We'll never know..."

"Yes, you're right," Anna said coldly. "It's impossible to know." She was growing tired of this game. There was no satisfaction in it. No one was going to congratulate her for figuring out that Professor Plum had been stabbed in the kitchen. *And to think, I came here to stop this creep from saving the world. The least I can do is to make sure that he doesn't fool the world into thinking he saved it. If I wait for my chance, I might be able to stuff this pillow down his throat. I can create an unfortunate by-product of my own.* Anna figured she could overpower the scientist. Or maybe she would just keep hold of him long enough for Ben to arrive. He was a soldier—she figured Ben would know how to kill. "So there is no second wave of eruptions—and no second set of nuclear weapons?"

"No, but the world is being bombarded by freak weather. There's a real nuclear winter to clean up, and people with radiation sickness to cure or contain. It's the Pottery Barn rule: you broke it, you own it. I own it now and I plan to fix it. I'm not about to let millions of people die just because some computer hacking bitch wants to get in the way! I'm the only one who knows what happened out there, so I'm the only one who can calculate the real effects. I understand exactly what is happening to our global climate and I know what we need to do to address it. That's what I do. I'm a scientist; I use my knowledge to help humanity survive." As he talked, a giant mushroom cloud filled the screen behind his head. Next, it showed smart bombs as they blasted into homes and schools, throwing body parts into the air. After that, gaunt, naked women and children walked underneath chemical showers.

"You are so small and insignificant. You can't possibly comprehend what you've gotten yourself mixed up in, but I do. Nothing is more important than this story, nothing matters more than tying up all of the loose ends and holding it all together. When those people out there stop believing in the same story the whole world falls apart."

Anna couldn't take it anymore. She ran across the room. "Fuck you!" she screamed, as she slammed into his chest. With the strength of someone who had shot men from close range with a pistol, Ulent hit back. He smashed Anna's jaw with the back of his hand. He grabbed her by the neck and spun her across the room and into the couch. She sprawled across it and struggled to move, managing to wedge herself back into a sitting position.

Ulent ran back to the desk and grabbed the pie up once more. He held it out in front of himself and snarled, "Try to mind your manners, won't you. I'd hate to have to stain my nice couch."

In her dazed condition, Anna wasn't sure why he would throw a pie at her. She did know that she had lost her cool and it hadn't helped. *You've got to be smarter than that. Keep him talking. Say anything.* Falling back to the couch she knocked one of the cushions forward. It revealed the last page she had been trying to read before she had charged across the room. Anna saw a word that Ian had mentioned. "You were born in Hyber … no, Hyder-a-bad?" Anna gasped as she read the syllables haltingly.

"So, you know about that too," Ulent began, when he realized that Anna had been looking behind the cushion as he spoke. He sprinted across the room wielding the pie menacingly in Anna's direction. Ulent knocked the cushion off the couch before Anna could stop him. "What is this? Crib notes?" Ulent declared as he turned to slap Anna once more. " I bet you were stupid enough to bring your only copies."

Anna fell off of the couch as she tried desperately to crawl away from the advancing scientist. He kicked Anna in the shin as she tried to move.

"Yes, so you know everything. I am a fraud. My real name isn't Oppenheimer; I stole that from someone they used to call the greatest scientist of them all. I'm not even from Ukraine. The best schools already had their quotas filled for my kind, so I became exactly what they wanted – a poor Eastern European orphan."

Anna used her arms to pull herself across the wood floor. She backed into the shadows of the hallway.

"I couldn't even get into this country using honest means. One of my brothers had to wear a dress just so they'd let us come here. I've come from nothing; I pulled myself up by my bootstraps. I'm the chief advisor to the president. I am the savior of the world."

Anna felt his bare foot bury itself in her side as he kicked at her again. Then he flipped her over with his foot and stomped down on her stomach. He held his one foot in place while he shifted his weight onto the leg that pinned Anna.

"In less than half an hour, a Presidential helicopter will be arriving to pick me up. It will carry me back to Washington, where I'll announce that the detonations went off as planned. At this very moment, people all over the world are praying. They're praying for me to succeed. They're praying that I'll figure out a way to save the world. And I've already answered their prayers. I've done what no god could ever do—I answered their prayers before they were asked."

As Ulent removed his foot, Anna sucked her breath back into her lungs. She realized her body couldn't take much more. She wasn't going to die lying on her back in this darkened hallway. From reserves of strength that she didn't know she had Anna grabbed hold of the wall and pulled herself to her feet.

"That's perfect," Ulent smirked. "It gives me a nice, clear shot, at eye level."

He pointed the pie at her once more. Anna had no idea why she should be intimidated by a cream pie, so she continued to walk. "I'm not afraid to use this, you know," Ulent barked. "There is no good. There is no evil. There is only knowledge. Knowledge is power. I hold all the power right now. I will kill you."

I'm already going to die. Anna thought. The realization that she was already in the process of committing suicide was comforting and it gave Anna the strength to keep walking. When she reached the back door Anna turned and looked directly into Dr. Oppenheimer Ulent's eyes, as she pulled it open, her eyes filled with defiance.

Ulent flung the pie forward. As if in slow motion, Anna watched as the cherry flipped off the cream and flew towards her face. It grazed her cheekbone. She looked up at the frame of the doorway and was amazed to see that the cherry had ripped a hole in the wood directly beside her face. It left a red stain.

She closed the door behind her. Under the ash filled sky, she found herself in the darkest night she had ever encountered. Anna stumbled forward across the back lawn and in the general direction of the drain through which she had originally crawled. Behind her she heard the door open and then Ulent's voice. He cursed her in the darkness. Then she heard a loud popping sound which she couldn't place. She heard the door slam shut again. She felt along the ground for the grate. When her fingers came across it, she pushed it aside and crawled into the hole in the ground.

VI - Out of this World

*A*nna wept. She had failed. In her state, exhausted and battered, she couldn't remember what she had failed to do. All she knew for sure was that Oppenheimer Ulent was going to save the world. She lay there, underground in the drainage tunnel, covered in filth, and wished for death. There was nothing left for her to do. Anna was entirely powerless.

The earth began to shake. Dirt fell upon Anna's outstretched body, as parts of the tunnel started to collapse. Dirt fell into her eyes and blew up her nose. A grinding roar filled the air. And all of a sudden, Anna was once more filled with hope. *Maybe I've been imagining it all—Ulent and the rest,* she mused. *Maybe the world is still going to end, but everything else has just been a sleepless delusion.* Joy filled her at these thoughts. She crawled out of the tunnel and pulled herself to a standing position behind the shed in Ben's old backyard.

Around her the night was made day, a furious wind tugging at her clothes and pushing against her body. A white light fell all around. She covered her forehead and tried to peer up at the source. Anna had just managed to make out the shape when it lifted high into the starless sky and was gone. Her face radiated happiness. This was something entirely unexpected and good. *Visitors from outer space have landed*, she realized. *They've come to conquer the earth from us.* She went running back into the house to let Ben know the news. Just in the nick of time—when all had looked lost—outside forces were intervening. The world could still be at an end. Her dream endured. She stumbled up the darkened stairway and felt her way into the upstairs room where she had left Ben. She paused to let her eyes adjust to the shadows. Her heart jumped when she saw what now lay in the child-sized bed. It was a giant glowing green slug. *This is what the spaceship left behind*, Anna realized. *I am in the midst of an encounter.* Anna approached the bed and knelt at the edge. She thought for another minute, then she realized what it was she wanted. *This is all there is*, Anna thought. *This is the only salvation for humankind; this is our resurrection.*

She reached out her hand and gently placed her fingers on a bulge that protruded from the creature's body, her fingers sinking into the slime that oozed off of its soft flesh. She pushed against it with her palm. The creature stirred. It slowly raised its body off of the bed and stood before Anna in the darkness. She knelt before it and raised her head upward to examine it. Anna wanted to remember this moment forever.

She saw that it had a variety of tentacles and appendages that stuck out all along its trunk. The moisture she had felt seemed to emerge from its highest point, a pinnacle that was covered in writhing white worms. In every way, it was beautiful.

The giant slug uttered a greeting that came from deep within its core. Two of its tentacles waved over the top of Anna's head as it swayed gently to and fro.

Anna lifted herself to a standing position. Uncertain but determined, she peeled away her sweatsuit. She unzipped her jacket, and with her cell phone still in the pocket, she tossed it aside. She kicked off her shoes. She swept off her sweat pants, underpants, and socks.

Anna stood in front of the creature, completely naked, and declared, "I'm ready now. You can probe me."

After watching Anna go into Ulent's house, exhausted, Ben had laid down in the kid's bed in his old room and waited for her to return. At some point, as the dark had thickened, he had fallen asleep. He had woken up with a start when he heard what sounded like a propeller rotating outside. When he turned to face the window he had seen a brightly lit helicopter briefly touch down and then lift up again.

Realizing that he had been sweating, he had peeled off his t-shirt and thrown it against the wall, underneath the window. Then, he had laid there in the darkness, trying to remember exactly where he was. But before he had a chance to sort it out, Ben had heard footsteps coming in through the doorway behind him. Frozen in fear, a silence had blanketed him and that was when he felt a hand touch the bare skin of his back. When he turned over, terrified, he saw that it was Anna who had returned, kneeling at his bedside. With that, everything came back to him with a start.

He tried to act calm as if a woman with him in his old room was a natural, everyday occurrence. Ben had stood, yawned, and prepared to speak. But before he had the chance, Anna was naked in front of him. She was looking into his eyes and said, "I'm ready now. You can probe me."

Ben's instincts took over. He didn't know much about this, but figured a good first step would be to remove his pants. He tugged at the military-issue belt but it wouldn't budge. In his excitement, he couldn't seem to get his fingers to pry the thing loose. So he sucked in his stomach and pushed down on the waistband as hard as he could. Slowly he pried the pants over top of his hips until they fell around his ankles. His army-issued briefs followed.

Anna noticed, for the first time, that the slug had coils. It unfurled them and let them drop to its base. She figured these must be what allowed it to move. *I bet it's graceful—it must float from place to place.* She pushed up against the trunk of the creature and it floated onto the bed. In one smooth motion, it lifted its coils and raised Anna onto the bed with it.

Ben felt Anna's hands against his chest. He lost his balance and fell back onto the bed. As he fell, his legs—still wrapped up at the ankles in pants and underwear—lifted and kicked against Anna's legs. She tumbled into the bed on top of him.

Anna landed with her head atop the slug's moist flesh. She opened her mouth and softly ran her tongue down the wet surface. It tasted salty. Considering its form, that was surprising. She put one of its tentacles in her mouth and kissed it. "Do you like this?" she asked.

Ben felt Anna's tongue on his chest and then on the fingers of his left hand. He heard her whisper, but he was lost in sensations he had never quite before experienced.

The creature's body seemed to be quivering. Anna took that as a positive sign. "How about this—is this good?" she asked as she took another of its glowing tentacles into her mouth. As she did this, Anna felt another tentacle, one that she hadn't noticed before, pressing against her breast. She lowered her mouth onto it.

Ben felt adrift in a wave of euphoria. He moaned.

Anna heard noises coming from deep inside the slug's body. She lifted her head once more and began to kiss every inch of its trunk. She worked her way towards the patch of worms on its pointy top. As she moved upward, Anna felt the neon tentacles—three of them now—investigate the front of her body. She adjusted one of them so that it curled around her nipple. As she did, she whispered, "You must be tired from exploring the galaxy. Just lie back and explore this body for a while."

Ben heard Anna's voice in his ear. He didn't have much experience with this kind of sex talk, but he desperately wanted to seem like he knew what he was doing. "I guess this Martian has found a way to communicate with Venus after all!" he exclaimed. Under normal circumstances, this would have been enough to end the evening. Any woman in her right mind would have realized that Ben had no idea what he was doing, after a comment like that. But this wasn't any normal night. The planets had all aligned in Ben's favor.

"Your language, I don't understand it, but it's beautiful," Anna breathed back. Then she took one of the slug's green tentacles and moved it between her legs where Anna felt it probe her.

"My, what big tentacles you have…"

Ben had no idea if this was how people always talked during alien sex play. He hoped so. The only thing he knew for sure was that he was fully aroused.

She repeated this procedure, with each of its tentacles, letting the glowing slug probe her deeply, until she was thoroughly satisfied. Afterward, she laid her head against its fleshy trunk. The slug seemed to have lost consciousness. A purring sound emanated from its core. Anna carefully reached down, over the side of the bed, and felt around on the carpet for her sweat jacket. When she found it, she fumbled some more until she grasped her cell phone. She pulled the phone back up. She pressed the button that caused the display to light up. It read "6:08 pm". Anna had been awake for 51 hours and 3 minutes. She set the phone back on the floor. *I finished my term paper, witnessed a volcanic eruption, took part in a riot, visited my old school, fought off red-eyed ghouls, survived an amusement park filled with blood-thirsty sex freaks, confronted an evil scientist, and made love to an alien life form,* Anna reflected. *It's time to sleep.*

VII

*E*arly the next morning, before Anna had awakened, Ben snuck out of the Star Traders decorated bed. He found her cell phone on the floor and wrote down her phone number. Then he dressed, went outside, and drove the Humvee back to the armory. As he walked into the commo shop, First Sergeant Halverson saw him and demanded, "Private, where have you been?" Without missing a beat, Ben replied, "I've been having sex, with a woman, all night long. And it was good—out-of-this-world good in fact."

"Yeah, right," Halverson said as he led the other men out of the shop and towards the drill floor. "Next time, call in. Don't think I won't report you."

"Yeah, right, sex with a woman, faggot. Only someone who is gay would have to constantly declare that he isn't," Rieck hissed at Ben, as he followed the First Sergeant out. "Everyone knows that."

"It's your fantasy, Rieck," Ben shot back. "You can spin it any way you'd like, and don't forget to wash your mouth out with soap. You should be ashamed of yourself for using that word so freely."

Major Withers, who had been watching the whole scene from the corner, walked up to Ben. He put his hand on the younger soldier's shoulder. "Look, son. The United States Army has a standard operating procedure for these things," the chaplain began. "The SOP is that first you report your fellow soldiers for harassment. Second, the MI unit comes in to investigate; but they look to see if you're a homosexual, not if your complaints are valid. Third, the unit gets wind of it, and they hold a blanket party. And, finally, you're discharged under a category that's other than honorable. This is the way it has always been done, ever since 'Don't ask, don't tell.' Now get with the program, Specialist."

···◆◆◆◆···

Sadly, the world was saved. Order was restored.

President Crupt became one of the greatest presidents to ever fill the office. A few people said so before almost everyone said so, and after a while everyone said so. Although not actually elected to serve, his time in office during the "End of the World" Crisis (EW Day) solidified his standing. After all, Crupt had helped America to weather the storms and to emerge stronger than ever.

When the rightfully-elected, deposed ex-president came back, he sued in an attempt to reclaim his office. The issue went to the Supreme Court, which was by then packed with the 14 judges that Crupt had put in place using an emergency Executive Order. The case was entitled "The Once-President of the Old United States versus the Supreme Leader of the new, more powerful United States of America." Crupt prevailed.

Then he won the next election. It wasn't even close. Crupt took more votes than any candidate in the history of the United States – even more votes than voters. It was fortunate that he held onto the office because there were many more crises to endure. There was the reemergence of dinosaurs (number 33, on the list of "51 Ways To End Your World") during his second term, a giant asteroid (number two) during his campaign for his third term, and a great thousand-year flood (number 47) during Crupt's fifth term.

Each time America, and the world, stood on the brink of disaster. Each time because of the brilliant leadership of America, the world survived. After a while, people near and far forgot that they lived in unusual times. The abnormal became the "new normal" as life went on.

Atop the lava that covered Vancouver, Camas, Battle Ground, and the rest of Southwest Washington, new homes were built, lawns were laid, trees were planted, parks sprang up, and roads were built to connect it all. In short, it was a building boom. Eddie Chandran—funded by his brother, Willie—went into the construction business. The investment paid off. He couldn't put up houses quickly enough to stave off demand. Eddie designed one housing development after another. He commanded a team of architects and engineers. At any given time he had 20 construction crews at his disposal. Eddie's company was the most sought-after business around. It seemed that everyone wanted to own a "Chandran" home.

He never forgot his near-death experience and to whom he owed his life. Eddie joined a Lutheran Church (not the ELCA wing, or the SDL version, but the LCMS group) and gave them a huge chunk of his newly acquired change. He became an elder—the most prized position to hold in the organization—and crusaded to have a church put on every corner in his new housing developments. Turns out he picked exactly the right moment to spearhead such a movement. It seemed that in the wake of having survived what nearly was the end of the world, nearly everyone had found religion. It was revival time in America, the likes of which hadn't been seen since the First, Third, Fourth, or Seventh Great Awakenings in American history.

Between frequent trips to Washington D.C., visits to various labs, or junkets to New York to speak to the United Nations, Ulysses—Eddie's oldest brother, the long-lost one who now went by a new name—would invite the whole family down to his Lake Oswego home for fancy dinners. There he would corner Eddie (usually in the study) and complain that the scientists weren't getting the credit they deserved for having pulled the entire earth back from the brink of disaster so many different times. He couldn't understand why people stuck to superstitions when true knowledge was at hand.

Ian Takki knew that he was one of the lucky ones to have survived. At the last minute, before the pack of bloodsuckers could devour him in the Hap changing room, a female member of the group had jumped between Ian and the clan. It was a scene that played out almost as if it had been stolen from the story of Pocahontas. This red-eyed woman had convinced the leader of the group (a gaunt, hairy man—who Ian later discovered was her father) to let this olive-complected stranger go free. Of course, the entire conversation had taken place via brain waves, so Ian hadn't known exactly what was said. The next thing he knew, he was being forced to take part in some sort of ritual marriage ceremony. It was at this exact moment that Ian discovered he truly did love this new blood-sucking bride of his—or, at the very least, he was deathly afraid of her (which is pretty much the same thing).

To explain it all, the press had first reported that these packs of wild people all just had cabin fever. This seemed to explain why they had emerged from mountain homes near the original eruption sites. Then the scientists had weighed in on the matter. They had declared that it was a type of pre-traumatic stress disorder. The idea went that all of the mountain people had known that Ulent was about to set off nuclear blasts near their homes, so they developed "anticipatory radiation sickness." It had all been psychosomatic—imagined.

Ian and his red-eyed ghoul wife had conceived a child. It was born with 2 heads—one was a programming genius while the other developed a gift for gab (both occasionally consumed live frogs). For this, the U.S. Government had paid Ian a paltry 2.3 million dollars—barely enough for one of the new Chandran homes – he just had to sign a contract agreeing to keep it all quiet.

Uncle Sam had been more generous with Ben Padgett. After he reported that his fellow soldiers were harassing him because they thought he was gay, a "Morale and Integrity" Unit was tasked to investigate the incidents. They discovered plenty of evidence of Ben's homosexual tendencies; his comrades in arms had a steady supply of information to this effect. They also seemed to have a full supply of army-issued socks filled with army-issued bars of soap the night (one drill weekend) when they all threw a blanket party for Ben. He was beaten almost beyond recognition. The very next day, Ben was expelled from the military. It seemed he had a lack of moral fortitude, according to the final paperwork, and so he was not fit to serve in his highly moral unit, in the highly moral army, that served the highly moral American people. The ugly beating aside, it had been the happiest day of his life. At last, Ben was free; or, at the very least, the remaining bonds were of his choosing.

Earlier that same month, Ben had convinced Anna that she should move in with him. They wound up renting a house together. Anna had been a foremost concern for Ben ever since that night when they had been thrown together unexpectedly, the day before the world was saved. When he found out that Anna was pregnant, Ben decided that he wanted to take care of Anna and the baby. He was after all a gentleman, in the old-fashioned, Cole Porter sense of the word. Ben assumed he was the father.

Anna knew better. She had never told anyone—Ben especially—about what had happened at Dr. Ulent's house and what she had encountered in Ben's old upstairs bedroom afterward. Although she never tried to set Ben straight, Anna knew the baby growing inside of her had been conceived as a result of her experience with a glowing slug visitor from another world. Despite her disappointment over having failed to stop the world from being saved and the fact that she had given up her attempt to die due to sleep deprivation, something positive had finally resulted. All things considered, she desperately needed to believe that her encounter with an alien being had spawned a new creature, a new form of life had been created; a son, she was sure.

On warm afternoons, Anna would sit out on the covered patio, that extended off the home she shared with Ben, and contemplate the world her child would destroy.

Acknowledgments

I gratefully acknowledge the editing and suggestions provided by Brandon G. Thompson for earlier drafts of this novel. His expertise improves my words, while his wisdom betters me.

Credit is due to Alexia Meier (who was the model) and to Jennifer Miller (who was the photographer) for contributing an image that was used in the conceptualization of the cover art. The author's photo was taken by Christine L. Panell. Rachael Knudsen provided expertise on the cover concept. Jason Andrew Bond gave shape to the preface. I am thankful for the assistance of each one of these individuals.

Good vibes go out to Scott Meredith. Meeting him—and learning about his success—inspired me to see this story through to publication.

Many thanks go out to the entire team at ElectricSoup-fortheSoul.com for assistance with creative development. I appreciate the abetment of Eric A. Manus, C.D. Panell, Ric Saumean, Rich S. Allpen, and Doc Euci Smarn.

I am forever indebted to Charlie Franco and the entire Montag Press family—notably Mara Korzen, Pete Peru, Edward Bonilla, Gary Petras, Paul d. Miller, A.R. Meyering (R.I.P.), James M. Wright, Nathan Elias, Mark Miller, Nick Perilli, Mike Sauve, S.S. Whitaker, J.W. Langley, Jonathan R. Rose, Walker Zupp, and Kathy L. Brown—along with so many others. You have made this dream come true.

About the Author

*C*haris is a world wanderer who lived for years in Trinidad as a child, resided in Hong Kong as an adult, but always winds up home on the Columbia River shores. They maintain a wildlife refuge for words that have developed consciousness at <ElectricSoupfortheSoul.com>. Their writings have been published widely, most recently in Defenestration, Land Beyond the World, Jokes Review, Corner Bar Magazine, and Aphelion Webzine of Science Fiction and Fantasy. Look for their next story in the upcoming *Strangely Funny IX* anthology, and their next novel, *Azzfapple: The Tech That Eats Us*, will be available soon!

Made in United States
Orlando, FL
01 July 2022

19319508R00114